MIDNIGHT MOON

////

J.R. RAIN

THE VAMPIRE FOR HIRE SERIES

Moon World

Published by
Crop Circle Books
212 Third Crater, Moon

Printed in the United States of America.

ISBN: 978-1544255354

Dedication

To Jason and Lee.

1.

"I trust that anything discussed between us will be held in the utmost confidentiality," said the uptight man sitting across from me.

"It will unless I deem otherwise."

"You mean, unless I give my consent."

"That's not what I mean nor what I said."

The uptight man, whose name was Charlie Reed, studied me long and hard. I didn't like to be studied long and hard, or at all. Studying me long and hard might bring into question, say, my particularly sharp nails. Or the fact that I didn't, you know, breathe. Or that I was presently not casting a reflection in my office window, or on my computer screen, or even on the glass of beading water in front of me.

Charlie Reed was an electrical engineer for

Raytheon. He was maybe forty-five years old. He was trim and well-groomed. He smelled good too. There were no laugh lines around his eyes. If anything, there were dark circles around his eyes, and actual bags too. The man needed a nap, like pronto.

"Ms. Moon, you don't seem to understand. I don't want my confidential information discussed with anyone."

"Duly noted, and I will do my best to comply."

"I'm not sure that's good enough. Can you give me any other assurances?"

"If I don't get questioned by the police, you should be okay. If I don't need to stop a crime, you should be okay. If I don't need to report you, you should be okay. That's all the assurance I can give you."

He sat back in my client chair, tilted his head to the right and took in some air from the position. He thought about my words, then he started nodding. "I get it. You're neither an attorney nor a doctor."

"Nope."

"So there's no client or patient confidentiality."

"None to speak of."

"And should you need to go to the police, or the police come to you..."

"I'll decide how much I will tell them, if anything."

"You've been in this business a long time."

"Ten years and counting."

"And before that?"

"I was a federal agent."

He nodded. His nerves were settling. He hadn't liked me asserting myself. Whether or not that was because I was a woman, I didn't know. Granted, I could have found that out easily enough. Yes, I'm one of those super-duper weirdos who can read minds. But I don't read minds willy-nilly. Mostly because doing so sort of opens up a mindlink, and sometimes my own personal thoughts get through to them too. As in, he could know what I was thinking. I didn't think Charlie Reed wanted to know what I was thinking.

I waited for him to process the information provided. While I waited, I noted his slicked-back hair and neat suit and perfectly manicured nails. Now he started nodding. He was coming around to the idea that he needed my help more than he needed to tell me how to run my business.

"Okay," he said. "Your terms are reasonable. And Detective Sherbet had good things to say about you."

"Did he mention anything about my uncanny knack for getting out of sticky situations?"

"No. But you are joking."

"I am, but I kind of do."

"Get out of sticky situations?"

"Yes."

"Good to know. He also said you were, ah, particularly qualified to help me with my, um, situation."

"That's a lot of 'ums' and 'ahs,'" I said.

Charlie rolled his head from one side to the next, which resulted in a number of pops and cracks. Next, he adjusted his position in the client chair, shifting from one cheek to the next, probably because my client chairs weren't too comfortable. Or maybe because the conversation had taken a direction in which he felt less sure-footed.

Of course, any time a client came recommended to me from Sherbet for my "particular qualifications," there were going to be a lot of "ums" and "ahs" and neck-cracking and butt-shifting.

"Ms. Moon. Do you believe in ghosts?"

2.

"Yes."

"So you've seen them before?"

"Oh, yes."

"Do you see them often?"

"Yes."

"Every day?"

"Yes."

"Do you see one now?"

"No, not now. My house isn't haunted."

"Where do you see them?"

"Just about everywhere else."

"Are you prone to delusions, Ms. Moon?"

"Would I know it if I were?"

He thought about that. "Maybe not. But you *think* you see them?"

"I *know* I see them."

"And if you were to come to my house?"

"I would see it, too, if it were there. I might even see a number of them, depending on how extensively your house is haunted."

"Have you always been able to see ghosts?"

"No."

"And one day, it just happened?"

"You could say that."

"May I ask what prompted this change?"

"You may not," I said. "But it's nothing you need to worry about."

He had settled in evenly on both cheeks, which was never a bad idea. The topic, I suspect, interested him enough to ignore his apprehension. And as he sat and studied me, I studied him, too. In particular, his strange aura. Never had I seen a completely red aura before. Just red. Pure blazing *roja*, as they say in Spanish. Why I felt a need to think in Spanish at that moment, I didn't know. Why his aura was red, I didn't know that either, but I felt it endlessly fascinating.

"Seeing ghosts on a regular basis..." Charlie shook his head. "I don't envy you, Ms. Moon." He was loosening up, which I liked to see. I don't do well with uptight. Still, there was something off about him, and I wasn't just talking about the massive bags under his eyes, or the weird red aura. He seemed... lost. Unsure of himself. It was the way he sat, the way his eyes sort of seemed to look through me. I would have guessed he wasn't all here, despite his earlier tough-guy act.

"Oh, ghosts aren't so bad," I said. "They mostly keep to themselves, except when they don't. Are you married?"

"Yes. I mean, no. Well sorta."

I waited.

"She left me four months ago."

"When did you start seeing the ghost?"

"About two weeks ago."

"Tell me about your ghost."

He did. The sightings were few and far between at first, and never did he see the ghost full on, which I found interesting. He could only see her from his peripheral vision, and then only in his hallway, which was adjacent, apparently, to his home office.

"Can you describe the ghost?" I asked.

"It's a she, and she's surrounded by blue light."

"Anything else?"

"Whenever I turn to look at her, she disappears."

I nodded, trying to understand, but couldn't. I said, "And you only see her in your hallway?"

"Yes."

"Is she doing anything?"

"Sometimes she appears to be standing."

"And other times?"

"Kneeling. But it's hard to say. I only get fleeting images of her."

"And you did say blue light?"

"I did, yes."

I considered dipping in his mind to see what he saw, but I suspected I would probably see soon enough firsthand, if he elected to hire me. Besides, dipping into his mind opened my own up to him, and that was never a good idea.

"Oh, there's one other thing."

I just loved when there was one other thing. "Go on."

"I only see her at midnight."

3.

Kingsley and I were at the brightly lit Mulberry Restaurant in downtown Fullerton. Perhaps too brightly lit.

"Don't you think The Cellar should be our hangout?" I asked, squinting, referring to the popular subterranean restaurant just down the street. "I mean it's dark and atmospheric and kind of perfect for two freaks like us." I pointed up. "These are Christmas lights, no? It's only September."

"They're not Christmas lights."

"They look like Christmas lights."

"They're a string of lights. Patio lights, I believe. They add atmosphere."

"And light," I said. "Lots of light."

"You are becoming sensitive even to artificial light?" asked my big (and hairy) boyfriend.

"Maybe. I hadn't thought about it."

"You're squinting," he said.

"I'm doing my best Clint Eastwood impression."

"Or not," he said.

"Is the light thing a problem?" I asked.

"Not for me, but it might mean there's a change going on in you."

"What sort of change?" I asked, but suddenly I didn't want to know the answer.

"It might mean the thing within you—"

"Elizabeth," I said, surprising myself when I corrected him with her name. I usually called her far worse.

"Yes, Elizabeth. It might mean she is, ah, asserting herself in ways you might not be consciously aware of."

"Asserting as in, taking over?"

"Not quite, but perhaps closer than before."

"Not over my dead body," I said. "Or my deader body. Or whatever."

"Wanna change the subject?" he asked.

"Very much so, yes."

He asked about my newest case and I told him what I knew, even as I stamped Elizabeth back down into the deepest, darkest recesses of my mind.

"Have you considered the possibility of a succubus?" asked Kingsley.

Yes, I might be undead and, to some, creepy as hell. I might have seen things that no mortal would ever want to see, but that sure as hell didn't mean I walked around with an Undead Dictionary app on my cell phone, although that wouldn't be a bad idea.

I said, "Suck a what?"

"Succubus. It's a beautiful female demon who has sex with men."

"How fortuitous," I said.

Kingsley gave me a huge, wolf-like grin. "I imagine the succubi were invented to explain a man's indiscretions."

"And later were summoned into existence for real," I said.

I had been told that we vampires—and no doubt the werewolves and Lichtenstein monsters and everything in between—had been summoned into existence because enough people believed. Belief was a strange thing. Belief conjured real things from the ethers. Belief brought forth monsters. And angels, too.

"And for women?" I said. "Is there a demon counterpart?"

Kingsley nodded. "The incubus. A male demon."

"How convenient. And for homosexuals?"

"Both succubus and incubus have been known to sleep with their own genders."

"And for the gender neutral?"

"Oh, I assume there's a gender-neutral demon out there too. Or on its way."

I grinned. "Ordered up by humanity."

"In a way," said Kingsley, who had been at this immortal game a good deal longer than I had, like seven decades longer. "But think of it this way, the Universe can't *not* deliver what man has summoned."

"Or woman. Go on."

"The summoning of new things is what keeps this universe from atrophying."

"Even new demon things?"

"Anything, Sam. If humans can think it, or want it, or believe in it, the Universe will deliver it."

"Like the devil," I said, recalling a conversation I'd had a few months ago with, well, the dark lord himself.

He nodded. "Speaking of the devil, literally, have you heard anything from him these days?"

"Nothing since our last meeting."

"At the train station?" said Kingsley. "When he blew himself up, so to speak."

I nodded. The devil, in a dramatic exit, had stepped in front of an oncoming train, and wastefully destroyed what had been a rather sexy bad boy host body, even if he had been a full-blown devil worshiper.

"And how's Anthony doing?" Kingsley asked.

"Still keeps to himself."

Our meals were served. Admittedly, the serving part took a while, as plate after plate was laid out before Kingsley. Steak and veal and chicken and fish. He'd already slayed the steamed clams, shrimp cocktail, fried calamari, and fresh oysters. I was fairly certain our table just tilted toward Kingsley. He would have it no other way.

I said, "That's one more plate of food than last time."

"You jest, but what can I say? I'm a growing boy."

And he was, literally. Except he was no boy. Not by a long shot.

I had just twirled the perfect bite of angel hair pasta onto my fork, with a small piece of meatball to cap it off, when Kingsley pushed aside the first of what would be many empty plates. One or two people were watching him. Next, he positioned the chicken pomodoro in the place of honor before him.

"I literally didn't see you eat any of that," I said, waving at the now-empty plate.

"Truthfully? I didn't either."

I grinned and took my first bite. As I ate, I thought of my son. Yes, he still kept to himself, and no he didn't want to talk about that day two months ago, when he'd been kidnapped by a local pack of werewolves, a pack who'd been keen to consume his rare blood type. Or, rather, his rare blood *legacy*. Such blood—my blood, too, and my daughter's and my whole family—had the added benefit of giving the consumer added strength and abilities.

Lucky us.

I was halfway through my first meal—and tasting enough of it to actually kind of enjoy it—when Kingsley pushed the last of his plates away. I knew he wanted to wipe his mouth with the back of his hand. I knew he wanted to belch, too. I knew he also wanted to slam his fist down on the table and demand more grog, or whatever the hell it was that conquering Viking warlords drank. Instead, he sat back and used his napkin and wiped his mouth discreetly, and reached for his glass of wine as if he hadn't just eaten seven full meals, as evidenced by the empty plates stacked precariously on one corner of the table.

"You've been quiet," he said.

"And you've been busy," I said, motioning to his stacked plates.

"No busier than normal. You gonna finish that?"

He hadn't gotten the sentence out before I pushed my own plate over to him.

"You're thinking about your son," he said between mouthfuls.

"Hard not to."

"The thing about the devil," said Kingsley, who didn't bother with the twirl method, preferring, instead, the shoveling method, "is that he can't win."

"What do you mean?"

"It's in his nature to lose. It's how..." Kingsley shrugged and took another bite and might have swallowed without chewing. "It's how he was constructed. Or, rather conceived. God's foil and all that. God's foil who can never win, no matter how clever or smart or handsome the devil is. Remember that, Sam. Remember, there's always a way to beat the devil."

4.

The house was big. Damn big.

This was the kind of street I should be living on. This was the kind of home I should be living in, too. My God, Danny had been an attorney. I had been a federal agent. We should have gotten a nice home. A big home, one that didn't shake every time Anthony guffawed and slapped the floor, which he was prone to do when watching TV or playing Xbox. A home that didn't creak endlessly, too. A home with, wonder of wonders, an attached garage. A home with a laundry room and more than one bathroom. My God, what I would give for two bathrooms. A shiny, new, beautiful home with a billiard room. Why not, right? I suddenly saw myself playing pool with Kingsley and Allison and Sherbet. Maybe that character Knighthorse, too, and his pals

Spinoza, Sanchez and Aaron King, who may or may not be Elvis. Maybe some of my other cop friends I'd met on any one of my hundreds of cases over the years. Funny how I had so many police and private eye friends. Then again, I always did gravitate toward good people, honest people, and hardworking people—people who fought for truth, justice and the American way. And yeah, I'm pretty sure I would be friends with Superman, too, if he existed. Of all my friends, only Fang didn't really mix. Or Dracula for that matter. Or the Alchemist, although I suspected he might shy away from such gatherings.

Lots of men in my life, I thought. And only Allison and Mary Lou to balance out all that testosterone. And Tammy, of course. Luckily, she was mellowing out as she got older. She was also taking her gifts a little more seriously, too. She often asked to help me when she could, recognizing her value to me and my cases. Having almost lost Anthony had been an eye-opener for her.

Yeah, I pictured all of these characters—and they were all characters, every last one of them— here at my big new house, playing pool, having a barbeque, talking shop, ready at a moment's notice to help those who couldn't help themselves, to fight the good fight and put themselves in harm's way to help a fellow human being.

"Would be a helluva pool party," I whispered as I approached the door.

It was nearly eleven p.m., which was our agreed-upon time. I'd spent the last two hours with Kingsley at his own estate, which itself was so big that even jealousy went out the door. After all, is one jealous of, say, an ornate museum? Or a glass shopping mall? Or a skyscraper? Hardly. One admired and moved on, and that's how I viewed Kingsley's own rambling mansion, with enough extensions and wings to form an entire flock.

We had, of course, spent the majority of that time in his bedroom. The poor guy had to work at it, as I wasn't in the mood, or feeling sexy. Hard to care about such things when the devil has targeted your son. But I eventually came around, and I'm fairly certain the big oaf finally got what he wanted. By the time I left, he was out cold, snoring away, and looking far more like a bear than I was comfortable with.

The community wasn't gated, nor was Charlie Reed's home. That said, it was hard to miss all the security cameras. He'd warned me about the cameras, which was why I had overdone it on the makeup on the way over here. At the door, I knocked lightly. He was evidently waiting for me, as the door opened immediately and my new client's now-familiar face appeared above me.

"Thank you for you coming, Ms. Moon," he said. "I would think these aren't your normal working hours, but I suspect private eyes work all hours of the night."

I winked and shot him a blank with my forefinger. "You suspect right."

He stepped aside and showed me the way in. My Asics made a surprising amount of noise on the polished marble floor. In the foyer, at the base of twin curved stairways, I was greeted by an alabaster statue of a rising horse pawing the air. Or whatever the hell they might call it in horse circles. I asked as much.

"Rearing," he answered. "I take it you're not a horse girl."

"Not really, although I do have an affinity for wolves."

"Sure," he said, and looked a bit puzzled.

"A beautiful home you have," I said. "Who knew electrical engineers made so much money?"

"We don't. But I just sort of have a habit of..." But he blushed and looked away.

"A habit of what?" I asked.

"Making money. It's weird. Everything I do, it just sort of works out for me."

"Lucky you," I said.

"I suppose. This way, Samantha. I can show you where she appears to me."

She being his ghost of course. I was led through the entryway and down a small hallway, then through the kitchen and living room. I noted the 90-inch TV hanging from the wall. Yeah, a lot of money. Along the way, I kept an eye out for any ghostly activity. To my eyes, ghosts appear as a collection of energy. And by energy, I mean the surrounding staticy energy that only I can see, energy that lights up the night for my eyes. The more the energy that's gathered, the brighter the ghost. As far as I could tell, there were no ghosts.

At an office that was surely fit for an ace detective, there was a desk of epic proportions. Not just U-shaped, but a complete wraparound desk, with a narrow opening that afforded access within. Once inside, Charlie no doubt felt that he could conquer the world. Or at least eBay, or whatever the hell he did in here. At any rate, this would make a helluva crime-fighting command center.

No less than three full computers sat on the interconnected desk. Two laser printers. Stacks of paper, folders, a Kindle, an iPad, another tablet computer of unknown origin. Trinkets and other knickknacks filled the remaining desk. Or tried to. There was, after all, a lot of desk space to fill up. Between two of the computers, I saw a complete Star Wars fleet of X-Wing fighters and flying bookends (which is what they always looked like to me), and other oddly-shaped spaceships that someone had spent far too long gluing together. *I'm looking at you, Charlie Reed.* There was the roundish Millennium Falcon, tilted at a proud angle, ready to unleash its full arsenal upon the forces of evil, which, I assume, meant Darth Vader, although Darth Vader was the star of three movies of his own.

There were other toys/figurines, too. Batman and Superman waging an epic battle, forever frozen on his desktop, each delivering an epic punch that would probably hurt. There was Wonder Woman with her long, Amazonian legs. I didn't have long legs, Amazonian or otherwise. I had short legs, and maybe a little too muscular, according to Danny back in the day. The dick.

"She appears there," said Charlie, sidling up next to me a little quieter than I was prepared for. Hard to sidle up next to me with my own super hearing, but he'd done it. Anyway, he was pointing to a side hallway through a nearby archway. Yes, the study was so big that it had two entrances.

"Mind if I have a look?"

He didn't mind, and so I did. The hallway branched to the left and right. The right dead-ended at a floor-length series of drawers and cubbyholes. The left opened into another bathroom. Neither end revealed a ghost, although I was sensing a lot of... energy in the hallway. I stood there and let it sweep over me, and sort of reveled in it.

"You see anything?" he asked.

"No ghost girl," I said.

"Well, that doesn't surprise me. We're early."

"Of course," I said, and stepped back into the office. "Which of these computers do you use?"

"This one here."

"Mind if I sit? Do as they do in Rome, as they say?"

"Sure," he said, pleased all over again that he seemed to be loosening further.

I moved over to it and sat down in it. Leather, with lower back support. A full array of paddles and levers underneath. Brass studs. High neck support. I veritably disappeared into it. Cozy as hell. How anyone could actually get any work done in it was beyond me. The sucker was just begging to be tilted back and slept in. Or meditated upon.

"You work from home?"

"Rarely."

"So this office..."

"Is mostly just for show," he said, and blushed a little, and I realized he'd made a small joke. If anything, the whole damn house was for show. Yes, he was definitely loosening up. "I am working on a novel, though," he added.

"Ghost story?"

He chuckled. "Actually, it's a fantasy novel."

"Fantasy? Like sexual fantasies?"

He laughed again. "More like a *Game of Thrones*, although there is sex in it. I try to make the story as real as possible. Except, you know, the dragons and shit."

"Right," I said. "Because dragons aren't real, of course."

"Of course," he said cheerily. Then he turned somber, literally on a dime. His red aura seemed to deepen to a crimson. "Except that I haven't written in four months."

I did the math. "Since your wife left."

He nodded. "Right. A world-class case of writer's block."

I looked at the time. We had about twenty minutes to kill before his very own Lady in White showed up. While we waited, I asked to read the first few pages of his novel. He didn't know what to make of the request. No one had ever read the book before. Not even his wife.

"What about the ghost?" I teased.

No, not her either. But that broke the ice and he asked me to move over a little, and I did, and he brought up the book on his computer. Then he moved away to sit at a full-length couch near the arched hallway entrance, where he watched me like a voyeur. I don't like being watched like a voyeur or otherwise, so I did my best to ignore him. Judging by the intermittent spitting sounds, I think he might have been chewing his nails.

I wasn't expecting much. In fact, I had already been planning on how to let him down easy if I thought the book sucked—including wiping his memory of me reading the book—when I came across something surprising. A remarkably fine first sentence that hooked me. And a second that might have been even better than the first. And a third that was rich and real, and so I kept reading. And reading. And as I read, something happened to me, something beautiful and magical, and not expected at all. I felt...

Transported. Straight into his fantasy world, where his characters came to life. They were funny and real and troubled and heroic—and that was all within the first twenty pages. A *Game of Thrones*, indeed. Maybe better. Maybe a lot better.

I didn't want to stop reading, couldn't stop reading. Charlie's fancy home had long since disappeared. Charlie had disappeared, too, until I heard his words reaching from seemingly far away. I blinked, irritated, wishing like hell that whatever was talking to me would just go away. I was, after all, quite happy here in the magical land of Dur.

Finally, finally, Charlie's words reached me.

"Sam, she's here."

5.

And so she was.

Crankily, I looked up and saw the bluish glow in the hallway. The glow was pretty damn obvious, more so than just about anything I had ever seen. No wonder why he caught snatches of it, even being a mere mortal.

Yes, I'd seen all levels of apparitions, from the very faint, to just blobs of energy. I'd seen more full-bodied spirits, too. My last interaction with Danny's ghost had been a particularly clear apparition. Little did I know at the time that the real Danny—as in, his actual soul—was hiding in my son.

Let it go, Sam.

I nodded to my own internal dialogue and let it go. For now. After all, a brightly lit ghost was presently standing just inside the hallway.

"You can see her?" I asked.

"Only when I turn my head and look away." He demonstrated for me. "I can see the bluish glow, and maybe, just maybe, a woman standing there. But when I turn to look at her—poof, she's gone."

Except, of course, I wasn't having that problem. There was no poof. I could see her full on, and she was quite beautiful. She wore a sort of nightgown, but it was antiquated. She was tall and slender and had big, nearly cartoonish eyes. Eyes that, if I had to guess, were filled with tears. She also seemed familiar in a way that I couldn't put my finger on. I'd certainly never been to this house before. Nor had I seen her. I was sure of that. No way anyone could forget a face like that. But yet... I felt I might know her. Worse, that I *should* know her. Was she an actress, maybe? A model? A pin-up girl from yesteryear?

That was about when my warning bell sounded, buzzing lightly in my head, and causing an increase in heart rhythm, which really wasn't saying much. But it was noticeable, at least to me. The buzzing was light, akin to a pesky mosquito. I was being warned that something was amiss, but not terribly so. His friendly ghost, I suspected, was anything but friendly. In fact, few things caused my inner alarm to sound. Vampire hunters, yes. Serial killers, check. The Devil himself? Oh, yes. Ghosts, not usually. Yet, here was my inner alarm, warning me of potential danger.

I continued sitting in the chair, surrounded by toys and computers and enough desk space for a start-up company, and watched the ghost standing in the hallway, staring forward.

Most important, I was pretty sure she wasn't a ghost. At least, not any ghost I had ever seen. The energy was different around her. Most ghosts were composed of zigzagging energy, a sort of gathering of such energy. Not her. She was complete, whole, pure. Just... not quite here. Closer to a hologram than anything.

I eased away from behind the desk, and stood. Charlie shot me a glance but, interestingly, the ghost never looked my way. In fact, if anything, she looked even more distracted, more distraught. Now I could see the tears spilling from her eyes. Most interesting—yes, most interesting, I could see her lips moving. Rapidly. She was speaking. Now she bowed her head. Was she praying... praying?

I edged through the gap in the desks, and got a better look at the woman standing in the archway. She was beautiful and otherworldly. She seemed to take no notice of me.

"It's okay," I said to her, now about halfway from the desk to the arched opening. "I won't hurt you."

But my words had no effect. She just stood there, lips moving silently, and weeping. Since when could I see a ghost's irises and pupils? I was pretty sure that was never.

Because she's no ghost, I thought. What she was, I hadn't a clue.

I saw her perfect, even teeth, her impossibly full lips. She didn't seem real, as in, no woman really looked like that, did they? She could have been a Disney princess come to life. Or any man's fantasy come to life.

Now she bowed her head and held her fingertips to her lips, and now I was certain she was praying. A second or two later, she turned around and walked away, disappearing within a few steps. And just like that, she was gone.

6.

I was in Detective Sherbet's office, and I had just given him Charlie Reed's address and he didn't seem too happy about it. He mumbled something about ghost hunting, and that he was a real detective, and that he wasn't paid enough for this shit.

"You know I can hear you, right?" I said.

Sherbet shook his blocky head, and took his mumbling internally.

"Every thought, too."

He input the address and clicked the mouse harder than he had to. He squinted at the screen and blew air through his nose that whistled if you listened hard enough. The screen reflected off his glasses, making his eyes appear bluer than they were. Sherbet and I had a wide-open channel. He couldn't lie to me to save his life. We were tight like that.

"Too tight," he said. "And my head isn't blocky. My wife says it's proportionate to my body." He caught my next thought before I could barely think it. "And, no, my body isn't blocky, either."

"I like blocky men."

"You're one weird chick. Okay, got the address. There's nothing here."

"No murders? No deaths?"

"Nothing at all, Sam. Wait. A domestic disturbance call was made in '92. But that's it."

"What were the names?"

"Helga Antigone reported her two sons fighting in the yard to police. Apparently, she hosed them down before the police got there. My kind of woman."

"Two brothers fighting in thirty-five years? That's it?"

"'Fraid so."

I said, "Just because nothing was reported, doesn't mean there wasn't a murder," I said.

"That's my girl. Always looking on the bright side."

"You know I'm right," I said.

"I'd like to believe a girl wasn't murdered there, but, yeah, you're right."

"Except..." I began.

"Except she didn't look like a murder victim," said Sherbet.

"No, she doesn't," I said.

"I can see her there in your thoughts. She's, um, quite the looker. She is dressed oddly."

"How well can you see her, Detective?"

"Well, I'm relying on *your* memory. And, like the memory of the giant Sasquatch on top of you last night, it's a little blurry, thank God."

I would have blushed if I could. Maybe the detective and I were a little too tight.

"You can say that again, sister. Anyway, the image kind of comes and goes as you think about other things. But I can see her there in your thoughts."

I nodded. Telepathy was weird. Seeing my memory had the transverse effect of creating his own memories. Sort of a watered-down memory. In effect, he now had a memory of something that he had never seen.

"About as weird as it gets," he said.

"What do you make of her?" I asked.

He leaned back, closed his eyes, either accessing his own memories or mine. To help him out, I brought her up in my own thoughts and tried like hell to keep her steady for him. Harder than it sounds.

"Beautiful, buxom. Nice figure, although kind of hard to tell in that gown. Little feet. Big lips, small ears. Eyes about as round as I have ever seen. Seems distraught. She also looks like she's praying."

"Praying. People still do that, you know."

I thought about that as he continued, "Mostly, she seems a little too perfect, if you ask me. Like she's not really real. I mean, no one looks like that, right? It's a bit like that movie... what's it called..."

"*Weird Science*," I said.

"Don't act so smug, Sam. You saw it there on the tip of my tongue. The point is, the beautiful woman in the movie, Kelly Le something or other—"

"Le Brock."

"Yeah, her. Anyway, she represented the *ideal* woman to two teenage boys."

I nodded, recalling the entity's eyes again. Her figure was hidden mostly in a nightgown of sorts, but I suspected it to be perfect under all those layers. "She did look like a walking, talking Barbie."

"Or praying," he added. "But yes, she's beautiful, but off. Not quite of this world."

"So what are you saying, Detective? That she's not real?"

"Not in our world."

His words hit home, and I found myself nodding. Not real in our world, but perhaps another world? As crazy as that statement was, I'd lived through enough crazy stuff to know there might be some truth to it.

"Or maybe she was a hologram or something. You said he was an electrical engineer. Maybe he gets his jollies creating, you know, computer programs or holograms or robots and shit. Maybe he was testing something on you? And being a 'paranormal investigator' made you an easy target."

I opened my mouth to laugh it off, but the truth was, Sherbet's logic made sense.

"And you yourself said you didn't dip too far into his mind," he added.

He was right. I hadn't, if at all.

"Well, there you go," he said, picking up the thought instantly. "Maybe you missed something. Maybe he was pulling a fast one on you. Testing out some new technology."

"Then why did my inner alarm go off?"

"Barely went off. You said it yourself. Just a small blip or two."

I nodded. Sherbet, as always, heard and remembered everything. "Yeah, I don't know what to make of that."

"Maybe your inner alarm thingy goes off if you find yourself in the middle of a prank."

I blinked at that. "Yeah, maybe."

"Well, I'm guessing it does. And I'm guessing your new client was having a little fun with you. Think about it, he had all the time in the world to set up that hologram in his hallway. Or whatever it was."

7.

"But that doesn't make any sense," said Allison. "Why on earth would he invite you over to his home just to prank you? And then give you money?"

"A lot of money," I said.

"Was his check good?"

"Very good," I said.

We were working out in Allison's gym in Beverly Hills, where she sometimes worked as a trainer. Gyms in Beverly Hills consisted of lots of chrome and shiny equipment. Lots of fake plastic boobs, too.

"Seems like an expensive and not a very funny prank."

"Unless it was filmed," I said.

"Which might be why your inner alarm was

bonging."

"Hardly a bong," I said. "Barely a blip."

"Well, maybe the detective is onto something. Maybe your inner alarm was warning you that something was off—just not something life-threatening."

I thought about that as I took my turn on the abdominal crunch machine. As usual, Allison slipped the key ring to the lowest hole on the stack. And, as usual, I crunched or lifted or pulled the heaviest weight with casual ease. Truth was, lifting weights did little for me, except getting me to sweat. And I always liked to sweat for some reason. Sweating felt so... human.

When I was done, I'd caught the attention of two older men. Both were chatting among themselves and looking over at us and no doubt working up the nerve to come over and hit on us. I gave them both a suggestion to mind their own business.

"Hey, they were kind of cute," said Allison.

"And I kinda have a boyfriend. Besides, they're way too old."

"How old?"

I slipped into their minds again. "Fifty-five and fifty-one."

"They sound rich!" said Allison.

"Oh, brother," I groaned. "Can we get back to the subject of me?"

"Yes, Your Highness. Lord help any of us if we happen to stray from all things Samantha Moon."

"That's better," I said. "And lose the attitude. You know you love to talk about me."

She opened her mouth to protest. Then closed it. "I do," she said. "Dammit, I really do."

"I know, sweetie."

"But I have a life, I swear."

"I know you do."

"Don't patronize me. I'm part of a triad of witches, dammit."

"I know you are. And it's a very, *very* powerful triad."

"You're such a bitch sometimes."

"Just sometimes?"

"Yes, just sometimes. If you were a bitch all the time, I wouldn't be your friend."

"Yeah, you would."

"Yeah, I would. And I hate myself for that. Just be nice to me, okay? Friends like me don't come around too often."

"Keep telling yourself that," I said, and was about to finish off my set, when I yelped and released the rubber grips, both of which had melted in my hands. Smoke hissed off my reddening palms. I looked at Allison and noted the wicked gleam in her eye, a gleam I didn't see often enough. I kinda liked it. In fact, I liked when she stood up for herself, even if it was standing up to me. Especially when it was standing up to me. White smoke curled up from her index finger, the nail of which still glowed softly.

"You were saying, Sam?" she asked.

"Nothing," I said. "Nothing at all."

***

We were having smoothies in the gym juice bar. Mine was heavenly, and I powered through brain freeze after brain freeze—all of which tended to last only a few nanoseconds—until I'd sucked down nearly all the smoothie.

"You didn't come up for air once," said Allison.

"Don't need to," I said.

"There oughta be a medical review board for people like you," she said. "I mean, actual verifiable studies."

I shrugged. "Would take the fun out of it, I think. It's kind of nice not knowing your limits. And what's with the 'people like me' crack? You're not too far off the mark, either, you know."

"I know. But witches are human, Sam. We live and die and make babies."

"I can make other vampires. Does that count?"

"Nope."

"Well, I can die, too."

"I know, Sam. But your death is... different."

I nodded. "There are some who say we cease to exist."

"By some, do you mean Fang?"

"Fang knows his stuff."

"Fang's a little too creepy for me."

"So says the witch who melted the rubber off the crunch machine."

"You had that coming, missy. Be glad I didn't melt off the tip of your nose, too."

"You're kinda badass for someone so needy."

"Jesus, will you quit saying I'm needy. I like you, dammit. And I like being your friend. Is that so needy?"

"Maybe I never had a friend like you."

"Well, friends can be needy. Get used to it."

"Am I needy?" I asked.

"Not often. But you will be, someday. And if so, I will be there for you."

"Jesus, are you trying to make me cry?" I said.

"Did it work?"

"No."

"Dammit."

"Back to the dying thing," I said. "Can you make heads or tails of it? I mean, why wouldn't I go to heaven, or even hell? Why would I cease to exist if, as they say, the soul is immortal?"

"I don't know, Sam. Is there someone you can ask?"

I thought about that. I doubted any of my mortal or immortal friends would have the answers. Ishmael, my one-time fallen angel, might have a clue. Then again, there was always—

"Automatic writing," Allison and I said together.

The juice bar was tucked away down a side hall,

which gave us some privacy. I'd already commanded the juice bar girl to forget anything she might overhear between Allison and me.

"You know that would be a great title: *The Ghost in the Hallway*."

"That was random," I said.

"I was thinking about your case. Hey, maybe I should write it. Do you think I would be a good writer?"

"Yes."

"Really?"

"Probably not."

"Such a bitch."

I chuckled at that. Truth was, one never knew who might be a writer... much less a good one. I would never have pegged Charlie Reed to be one of the better ones, and yet his book had been so rich, so beautiful, so alive...

"Oh, I want to read this book!" said Allison.

"Join the club. It's not finished. I'm not finished with it either. Still have a few hundred pages to read."

"And it's a fantasy?"

"Yup."

"Like a sex fantasy?"

I shook my head. "Sword and sorcery."

"I'm not really into that."

"You like *Game of Thrones*?"

"I love *Game of Thrones*—oh wait."

"Bingo," I said.

"It's like that?" she asked.

"Better."

"Okay, now I really have to read this book!"

"Get in line, sister. Meanwhile—"

"Meanwhile, you want my impressions of the ghost, too."

"I do, yes. And why are you smiling?"

"I just love when you need me."

"Oh, brother."

Allison grinned and closed her eyes, no doubt probing the crap out of my mind. Her own mind was permanently closed to mine, as one of the witches in her triad considered me—or, rather, vampires—to be their enemy. And she might have a point. The demon bitch inside me was very much their enemy. She was, quite, frankly, *everyone's* enemy, which is why I did all I could to bottle her up, especially since Elizabeth herself could hear and see everything I could hear and see. She was dangerous if ever let loose. And each day, while I slept, she *was* let loose, slipping out of my physical form to join her fellow dark masters... somewhere. Where, exactly, I didn't know. But it was another world, I think. A parallel world, perhaps.

"Your mind is busy, Sam."

"Ya think?"

"Okay, I found her. Yes, she is beautiful. Wow. And that nightgown. It's old, Sam. Real old."

"How old?"

"Medieval maybe. Either way, her dress isn't

from around here. And probably not from this time, either."

"Maybe she was killed at a renaissance faire or something?" I asked.

"Maybe."

"But that doesn't really explain her unreal appearance."

"Jealous much, Sam?"

"I'm not jealous. Did you have a look at her eyes, her mouth, those long legs?"

"I did, Sam, and she's beautiful."

"Don't you think they are just, I dunno, a smidge off?"

"Maybe. Maybe not. I am only getting, at best, a now slightly blurry memory from you. Hell, even you are beginning to doubt your own memory of her."

Allison was right about that. The more I thought about the "ghost," the more I questioned what I had seen.

"You need to see this ghost again, Sam. And maybe you need me to tag along with you."

"You're half right," I said.

Allison scrunched her eyebrows together, then stuck out her tongue at me. "You're mean."

"What do you expect from a bloodthirsty fiend?"

"Fine, whatever. I just think you could use me— wait! You're going there tonight."

"I am."

"And you want to be left alone so that you can read that damn book."

"You caught me."

"Let me come, Sam. Pleeeease. I will be good. I just wanna read a few chapters. Puh-lease!"

"You sound worse than my kids."

"Please, please, please!"

"Fine, you can come."

She threw her arms around me and gave me a big fat kiss on my cheek.

"Gross," I said, wiping it off with the back of my hand.

"You're telling me. It was like kissing a dead—"

"Don't say it," I said. "Or I won't bring you tonight."

"Fine."

"Don't think it either," I said.

"I already did."

"Now who's the bitch?" I asked.

8.

With the events of the last few months, events that had made national headlines, Tammy had made it a point to pick up Anthony from school each and every day.

This was both sweet and scary and rewarding for me. Rewarding to see their bond growing. Scary because I was not there to do the picking up part myself. And sweet because it freed up my afternoons. I knew his school had installed even more cameras and added three or four security guards. The security guards were privately keeping an eye on my son. I knew this because I had commanded them to do so. My son was about as safe as a boy could be at school.

Additionally, Archibald Maximus, the alchemist to the stars (that's a joke) had since forged magical rings for my kids, rings that would render their "silver cord" invisible. A neat trick. Now, the baddies out there who feasted on the pure Hermes bloodline of little Light Warriors, couldn't find them. Nor would other Light Warriors, too, but that was less of a concern. The bottom line was: my kids were safe, their auras were hidden, and I could breathe easily again.

For now.

And what had become of the teacher behind my son's abduction, the sick bastard who had planned to watch the whole bloody show from high above? Well, he had disappeared completely... only to reappear in Kingsley's safe room. And by safe room, I meant safe for the rest of us. Kingsley, with each full moon, was about the biggest and baddest werewolf alive, and the teacher, as far as I knew, had been torn to shreds, since Kingsley preferred his meat rotten, not fresh. Undoubtedly, Franklin had long since burned the man's remains.

The werewolf pack that had gathered that night to feast upon my son had all met nasty ends, too, thanks primarily to my son—and thanks to the entity my son had summoned, the Fire Warrior. My son still wasn't right, and I didn't blame him. After all, he had killed those who wished to do him harm. Werewolves were men, too, after all. And this haunted my son to no end.

I also knew Anthony hadn't fully come to terms with the fact that he had, in effect, switched bodies with another entity, an entity he fully controlled. Hell, I wasn't fully used to it either, with Talos. That the entity he became seemed to be an unstoppable warrior that wielded a fiery sword and stood nearly ten feet tall was all sort of badass that, at present, was lost on my son. He would come around, I knew. Someday, he would understand that in our world—the world of freaks and monsters— that it was kill or be killed. And he had lived to fight another day. Nothing wrong with that.

Then again, that my thirteen-year-old son would have to live by such a motto was a terrible price that I paid every day, over and over and over...

At present, I was sitting in my minivan—not very far from where I had just downed a smoothie in record time. My windows were cracked enough to let in the fresh air, but not so much that anyone could overhear the conversation I was about to have. That is, a one-sided conversation, with me doing the talking and my hand doing the writing.

Who did the writing remained to be seen. In the past, it had been everyone from my spirit guide named Sephora, to a highly-evolved master named St. Germaine, to even an entity that I considered Mother Earth. So, truthfully, I hadn't a clue who would come through—or if anyone would. Since I hadn't used automatic writing in a while, I wasn't sure who I was plugged into these days, quite frankly.

I kept a small notebook in my purse, not for

automatic writing, but for taking statements. I clicked on my pen and opened my small notebook to a blank page. I moved the pen to the top of the line and closed my eyes and heard a small breeze force its way into the cracked window. The same breeze then moved over the skin of my arm. Of course, I could have been sitting here with the windows rolled up, but I liked fresh air, even if I didn't have to breathe it. Fresh air was comforting and, well, yummy.

The bitch inside me didn't like words like *yummy* or *fresh*. I could sense her discomfort, like a curmudgeonly old woman trying to get comfortable in a new recliner.

Hey, you picked me, lady, I thought.

Indeed, greater forces were at work as to when and how and why I was chosen to be a vampire. In the big picture, I was the perfect confluence of bloodline and reincarnated witch and, well, I was also kind of a badass in this life too. In the smaller picture, I had been set up by my angel and an old vampire for reasons unknown to me to this day. Of course, that same old vampire was now dead, thanks to a silver arrow from a vampire hunter named Rand. But my angel was still around. Maybe I would ask him someday.

Either way, I had been viciously attacked and seemingly left for dead. But I hadn't died. Quite the opposite. I had lived, and, from all appearances, I would live forever. Or, rather, had the *potential* to live forever. A silver bolt in my own heart would readily put an end to any talk of immortality.

"And then what?" I asked. "What happens to me then? When I die?"

As I asked the question, I emptied my mind. I even locked away Elizabeth good and tight. I didn't need her influence. I needed real answers. It was time.

I wasn't sure how long I sat there in the front driver's seat, just outside the YMCA, with the occasional person walking by, sometimes accompanied by the rattle of a dog's tags on his collar, or the squeaky wheels of a stroller. I was reclining back, but not all the way. The notepad was positioned on the center console, my hand hovering lightly over it. The hovering over it part was what kept me from falling asleep, no doubt. This was midday. I should have been asleep.

More time passed and I nearly gave up on the automatic writing. Maybe it didn't work for me anymore. Maybe it had never worked. Maybe it was always just my own subconscious talking to me. Or maybe it had been Elizabeth talking to me. No, it hadn't been because previous sessions had dealt with love and forgiveness and hope. Anyone who cringed at the word *yummy* would flee for the hills from the word *love*.

I had just made the decision to sit up when my hand twitched. I knew that twitch. I'd felt that twitch in years past. I waited and focused my breathing and calmed my mind further, and, after a few minutes, my hand twitched again. Then again. And now I felt a slight pressure as the tip of the pen was guided down to the paper, and my hand went from twitching to flowing as the words came out.

I cracked my eyes open and saw two words at the top of the page, two words that flowed in beautiful penmanship. Perhaps even *perfect* penmanship.

"Hello, Samantha."

9.

"Hello," I said aloud, feeling a little foolish talking to my hand.

A strong tingly sensation came over my entire arm, and I watched, with amazement, as words flowed from the pen and into my notebook. "You have some questions for me, I see."

"Questions, concerns, complaints..."

"Complaining only brings more of the same," wrote my hand, after being galvanized by what was, in essence, small electrical impulses firing upon various muscles primarily in my forearm. The sensation was not unlike when Kingsley massaged my arms, his touch surprisingly soft, considering his skillet-sized hands. Of course, Kingsley's hands didn't stay long on my arms or shoulders—or on anything that wouldn't be hidden by a bikini.

The difference here was that I could actually see the muscles in my forearms being stimulated. I watched them undulate and quiver and spasm and pulse. All while my pen flowed, seemingly with a mind all its own over the notepad.

I said, "Well, I either complain now or forever hold my peace."

"And forever is a long time for a vampire."

"And even longer for a *dead* vampire," I said. "First off, with whom am I speaking?"

"A good question, Sam. I go by many names."

"Well, pick one, preferably one that I can pronounce."

"Let's go with Jack."

"Jack?"

"Yes."

"Just Jack?" I asked.

"I could pick another—"

"No, Jack is fine. We'll go with that. So, Jack, what are you? An angel? My spirit guide? A highly-evolved master? Father Time?"

"Yes," wrote my hand.

I waited, but apparently, that was all I was going to get.

"Just 'yes'?"

"Yes."

I thought about the implications. "You are all of these things?"

"All of it and more."

"You are... God?" I asked, and now I knew,

without a shadow of a doubt, that I had gone mad. Who talks to God? And through their hand, no less? Crazy people do, that's who.

More words appeared on my pad of paper: "What if I told you we are all God?"

"I would say that's some New Age gobbledy-gook."

"Then I'll just say this, and leave it: there is a very good chance I am God."

"That's it?"

"It's the best answer for you, now. After all, only crazy people talk to God, right?"

"Er, right."

"So let's just leave it that I *could* be God."

"Or you could be the devil."

"The devil exists within God, Sam. As do you."

"So the devil is God."

"You said it, not me."

"Are you playing with me?"

"I'm softening a difficult concept."

"That the devil is also God?"

"Yes, Sam."

"Most people believe the devil is a fallen angel."

"In such cases, they would be right."

"Because what they believe is true for them?"

"In essence, yes."

"The devil told me he came into existence because he was summoned into life, to fulfill a need."

"That would be closer to the truth."

"Does the devil tempt man?"

"The devil seeks to continue his existence."

I said, "So he needs to tempt man, he needs to promote evil. And he needs people to believe in him and hell."

"A complicated existence, to be sure."

"A group of people can really summon an entity into existence?"

"A group, yes. And sometimes just one."

I blinked at the words on my page, absorbing them, realizing I had been speaking and writing in a sort of trance. I said, "He seems particularly powerful."

"He has as much power as he is given."

That made sense, but I circled back to one of the original statements. The neat thing about automatic writing was that I could just go back and read through the dialogue. "You said you were softening a difficult subject. The subject was that the devil was you."

"Yes, Sam."

"Is this because all things come from you?"

"Indeed."

"All people, all life, all heavenly beings—"

"You say heavenly, I say nonphysical."

"Nonphysical—and everything else in the Universe—"

"Multiverse," my hand wrote, effectively cutting me off. "There are far more universes than this, Sam."

"All of this and more are from you?"

"Funny you should say 'more.'"

"Was that the wrong word?"

"It was very much the correct word. I am ever evolving, as are you. As is everyone, including the devil, including your universe itself. You could say that the very purpose of life is to expand into places not yet known or believed or conceived."

"But aren't you, you know..."

I tried to wrap my brain around the concept, and paused. My hand waited patiently. I tried again, "But don't you know *everything*? Don't you already know what you will expand into?"

"A common misconception."

"So God doesn't know the future?"

"God is aware of potentials. God is delighted when God is surprised."

"Who the hell can surprise God?"

"The surprise is in the potentials, Sam. And when one potentiality opens, hundreds, if not thousands more spread from that. And they continue spreading as each life is lived, as each decision is made, and as each and every person grows into his own. Everything expands. It is the point of existence."

"You said that. And darkness helps the expansion?"

"Even darkness expands, or what is perceived as darkness."

"And it all expands within you?"

"That is safe to say, yes."

"This is weird."

"Tell me about it."

I laughed. "I spoke with you a few years ago."

"You speak to me every day."

"Okay, but I'm referring to a conversation I had on an island, when I found myself sort of above the universe itself, adrift on a sea of space and time, in the presence of something... epic."

"Okay, now you're just buttering me up. You had a vision of me, yes."

"I had a vision of other dimensions, too."

"Indeed."

"Why?"

"It is how you reach God, Sam. It is how you find your way to me. You will need this information later."

"Later, when?"

"That is determined within the potentialities."

Okay, that was a little weird. I reread the words on the page before me. So many questions. Finally, I settled on, "Do you oversee everything, all life, all worlds?"

"Not quite. I *immerse* myself into everything."

"But don't you, you know, have a say in what's going on in your playground, so to speak?"

"My greatest joy comes from watching the expansion of life, without interference."

"Well, I think you might want to step in and sort

some of this crap out."

"What crap, Sam?"

"Life. The creeps out there. The evil bastards hurting other people. The dark masters who control and kill and destroy."

There was a pause. I'd gotten myself a little worked up. I was suddenly sure I wasn't talking to God. How could God not take a more active role in the lives of people, mortal or otherwise?

"Sam, let me begin by saying that yours is a free-will universe, a universe based primarily on attraction."

"Which means?" I asked.

"It means people get to sort it out themselves, without interference from me."

"You are here now. Is that not interference?"

"You are asking the big questions, Sam. I am here to give you the big answers."

"You're saying that no one else can provide me the answers I'm seeking?"

"Your questions are without precedent."

"You're telling me no one has asked these questions before?"

"Few, and those who did didn't do so with the expectation of receiving the answer."

"Because this is also a universe of attraction," I said aloud, "I attracted the answer. I attracted, in essence, you."

"Yes."

"And it is not interference if I am seeking you

out."

"You did not seek me out, Sam. You expected. Seeking and expecting are two different vibrations."

"I was just looking for answers. I wasn't looking for God."

There was a pause, and I nodded.

"Except we are all God."

"Aspects of God, yes. Children of God, yes."

"And sometimes the answer needs to come from the source itself," I added.

"I couldn't have said it better myself. Now, speak the question that's heaviest on your heart."

"You already know it."

"Stating the question prepares one for the answer. It paves the way, so to speak."

"Fine," I said, and collected my thoughts. "When I die, do I..." My throat clenched tight. With my free hand, I reached over and cracked the window for more air. I suddenly needed it for reasons I couldn't explain. *Old habit*, I thought. I noted two homeless guys who had gathered on the sidewalk in front of a bakery not too far from me. They were already hunkered down and sleeping. How long had I been sitting here? Surely no more than ten minutes. But maybe longer.

Refreshed and cleared-minded—or as clear as I could make it—I said, "If I die, do I cease to exist?"

10.

One of the homeless guys held an empty McDonald's cup up above his head, even though he appeared to be sound asleep. He had no takers. People pushed babies by—or jogged or walked by, his cup ignored.

My hand twitched and twitched, spelling the words: "First of all, Sam, I am going to give you some information that you did not know before."

"Well, duh," I said. "That's why I'm asking. And did I just say 'duh' to God?"

"You did."

"I'm sorry?"

"Is that a question or an apology?"

"Both?"

"You did it again. And you were right: that was a 'duh' moment. I should have elaborated. I am going to give you information that was not asked, but relates to your question. Such information could be misinterpreted as me interfering."

"Look, God, or Most High, or Almighty, Jehovah, Hosanna, the Big Guy in the Sky... whatever your name is. This whole *not interfering* business was your idea. Not mine. If you want to help me, feel free. Lord knows I need all the help I can get."

"The Lord does know, and you don't need as much help as you might think."

"Is that your idea of a pep talk?"

"It is truth. You have within you all the answers you will ever need."

"Except the answer about what happens to me when I die."

"Oh, it's in there too."

"Then why am I talking to you?"

"Because you don't believe it's in there."

I thought about that, and shrugged. "Okay, you got me. I guess I don't believe it's in there."

"Which leads to my earlier statement."

"The part about you giving me information that might be construed as interfering?"

"Yes, Sam. That part."

"I'm all ears," I said, looking at the pad of paper. "Or eyes."

Triggered by the softest of electrical impulses, my pen spelled out: "First off, you give the entity within you, the one called Elizabeth, too much credit."

"How so?"

"You attribute your great strength to her, and this is a fallacy."

"And what's the truth?"

"Much of your strength is yours alone, including your ability to connect telepathically and to teleport, among other things."

"I don't understand..."

"You have been selling yourself short, Samantha Moon. You believe you are beholden to her because of the gifts she has given you. In truth, she has given you very little."

I opened my mouth to speak, closed it again, then said, "I just assumed..."

My hand jerked, my fingers pulsed. "Of course you assumed, Sam. And the entity within you allowed you to assume. She wants you to recognize her as something greater than you, so great as to bestow upon you supernatural gifts, along with her darker needs."

"So the darker needs are all hers?"

"Mostly. It is, however, a true symbiotic relationship. She has awakened the darkness within you, too, and you don't necessarily hate it."

"Is that wrong?" I asked. "To not hate one's dark side?"

"There is no wrong or right in a free-will universe, Sam."

"But liking the dark feels wrong."

"Your experiences in life have helped you

define that feeling. The entity within you finds the darkness appealing, exciting, intoxicating. She can't understand why you do not see it as she does."

"Because I feel love, too," I said.

"She feels love, in her own way."

"A love for darkness," I said.

"In essence, yes. And she would not be wrong for having that love."

"For her," I said.

"It is the path she chose. But she is part of you, too. And she has considerable influence over you."

"Fine," I said. "That still doesn't explain all the telepathy and teleporting, my strength and speed—and all things weird and freaky."

I sensed the entity—God, perhaps—nodding his great head, although that was surely my imagination. "You died ten years ago, Samantha Moon. You are alive today thanks to the tainted blood you consumed, blood that both killed your physical body and held you in a sort of suspended animation, long enough for another entity to slip inside. But something else occurred, as it does with all of those of your kind. Your soul *also* poured into your physical body, completely and fully."

"And it wasn't completely and fully in my body before?"

"Oh, no, Sam. The soul typically resides in both the energetic world and the physical world at once. You were, in essence, in two places at once."

"And this is the case for all humans?"

"Indeed, although some dear hearts can reside in three or more places at once, depending on the needs of the soul."

"But why?"

There was a long pause, and I sensed the entity controlling my hand was gathering its thoughts. Or perhaps it was, you know, big on pregnant pauses. Finally, the pulse came and my fingers twitched and shimmied across the page.

"Sam, it is safe to say that all are connected to me. All are *from* me. All are *of* me. What's more, the aspect of the soul residing in the energetic world is *directly* connected to me. It is, in fact, an immediate extension of me."

"I'm sensing a *but* here," I said.

"It's a big *but*," wrote my hand.

"Nothing wrong with big butts," I responded, but already, I was dreading what might come next.

"No need to dread," wrote my hand, keenly aware of my thoughts. "But this might rock your world."

"My world was rocked ten years ago," I said. "Everything else is just minor aftershocks."

"Very well. A good outlook to have. I can see you are on steady ground."

"As steady as I can be. Hit me with your best shot."

"The very act of becoming a vampire drew your soul, in its entirety, from the energetic world and into the physical world."

I let the written words sink in, and when they did, I finally nodded. "And heaven is in the energetic world."

"Yes, Sam."

And then it hit me like a ton of bricks. "I am no longer connected to you."

"No, not like before."

"That makes me sad," I said.

"You are missed by me as well, but there is an upside here."

"And what's that?"

"You have become, in essence, your *own* creator. A free radical, if you will."

"What does that mean?"

"It means your soul has never been more alive, or more powerful. It means that you can fully utilize *all* the creative abilities I have granted all souls."

"All souls?"

"Few have mastered such gifts. The soul's ability is astronomical."

"Because its essence is you."

"Yes, Sam."

"And now my soul is fully contained here, within this five-foot, three-inch body."

"Indeed. And it is veritably exploding with possibility."

"This is a lot to take in."

"I imagine so, but remember: you have been utilizing your soul's many gifts for a number of years. You've just been giving credit to the wrong person."

"I gave all the credit to her," I said.

"This is correct. But without her, you would not be that which you call a vampire."

"She helped create me—"

"That is all, Sam. She helped create you. Nothing more, nothing else."

"But I feel less. The sunlight. Food. My reflection. These gross nails..."

"Spillover, yes. But nothing more. You are a powerful spirit, Sam Moon. A powerful creator. And someday soon, perhaps you will recognize that."

I sat quietly and looked at the words that had appeared on my page, written in a tight, neat script that I didn't recognize as my own. I had gone through five pages already. I placed the tip of the pen at the beginning of the next blank line.

I said, "So if I'm hearing you correctly, I have been ejected from heaven."

"You are living your heaven *now*, Sam."

I looked around at the mostly empty street, the two bums, the crow on the branch nearby. The sparkling facades of far too many high-rise apartments.

"It doesn't look like heaven."

"There is a kind of heaven in all things, if you choose to see it."

I sensed the wisdom of the words, but I wasn't ready to hear it. Not yet.

"You never answered my question," I said. "What happens when I die? Me. Samantha Radiance Moon." I rarely let slip my full name, as it is quite a mouthful... and begs too many questions. Yes, my parents were hippies. Growing up, my full name had been Samantha Radiance Sundance. You can imagine my parents' delight when they learned I would be marrying a Moon. Giddy would have been putting it mildly. Yes, Samantha Sundance had married Danny Moon. Our wedding invites had promoted the celestial theme. As had the entire wedding itself. It was a match made in the heavens, we had announced. I had thought so, too. Little did I know then that there would be no heaven for me...

I said, "And what happens when this physical body of mine should die? This vessel that contains all of my soul?"

"You will return to me, child, where you will re-emerge into all that is and all that will forever be. Where you will be loved by me forever more."

Tears flowed as I considered the words. Truthfully, I didn't know what to make of them, but knew exactly what to make of them, too, and I felt love for me unlike anything I had ever felt in a long time, and the dark entity within me shrank and cowered in the deepest recesses of my mind.

Minutes later, when I had cried myself out, something was tugging at my mind—no, my heart—something persistent and childlike and innocent, something that grew brighter even when I shined a light on it. I almost didn't ask. I almost didn't want to know. But I did want to know, too. Very much so.

"What is heaven like?" I asked. "Can you... can you tell me what I will be missing?"

"Do you really want to know?"

Through my window, I noticed one of the homeless men had awakened and was watching me. He looked familiar. Very, very familiar. I said aloud, "I think so, yes."

There was a pause. My hand twitched, then stopped. Twitched again, then lay unmoving, like something forgotten and broken. Finally, like a spider rising from the dead, it rose up and pulsed to life, and spelled out the words:

"Perhaps it is better if I show you."

My eyes widened at that, and I stared at the words spelled out before me for a heartbeat or two. Then I nodded, and said, "Yes, I'd like that. I'd like that very much. But how..."

And just like that, I was no longer in my minivan.

I was somewhere else, somewhere beautiful, somewhere majestic and free and untethered and light. It was somewhere not here, but it also didn't feel much different either. I saw people and buildings and activity and excitement and love. Mostly I saw love. And by my side was a little man I remembered, a little man I had met years ago at a Denny's, a little man who held my hand and pointed and spoke softly and laughed often and showered me with more love than I'd ever felt before.

It could have been hours or days later when I found myself seated once again in the minivan, my face in my hands and tears streaming through my fingers.

On the notepad before me were the words: "You are loved more than you know, Samantha Moon. Yes, you are loved very much indeed."

When I finally looked up, I noted the homeless man was gone.

11.

Tammy didn't like her dad very much.

Now, as she lay in her bedroom, with her mom in the next door office and her brother in his bedroom down the hall, she decided right then and there that she didn't like her dad at all. Nope, not one bit.

Tammy knew he had cheated on her mother. She had relived every lurid detail in her mother's memory. Tammy liked the word *lurid*. It made her feel grown-up to use it. She very much wanted to be a grown-up. Yes, she had recently turned sixteen, but she had lived far more than her sixteen years, she was certain. Even if the lives she lived were through other people's memories.

A few months ago, when Kingsley had come over, she had dipped into his mind and relived nearly every worthwhile memory the man had had. And that man had *lived*—and fought and killed... and made love. The many, many women he had made love to! Tammy smiled. She was still a virgin, yes, but reliving some of Kingsley's more titillating memories had been, well, wild.

Too wild for a girl her age, she suspected.

But, as she liked to believe, she was beyond her years, thanks to the thoughts and memories of these crazy-ass adults around her.

Allison had been a stripper in her twenties. A stripper! The stories Allison could tell, if she chose to tell them. But Allison didn't. She kept her past in her past. And, my oh my, the vampire boyfriend she'd had before meeting her mother. Wow wow wow! So hot. A boyfriend who was now dead, sadly.

Tammy relived that too.

Tammy could "relive" any memory of anyone around her, and she could do it quickly. She had developed an ability to "touch down" upon only the highlighted memories, so to speak. She'd never really explained this before, to anyone, but Tammy, when she dipped effortlessly into anyone's mind, could see that certain memories were "highlighted." She quickly learned to target these memories, as they were always the more interesting and worthwhile memories.

In the beginning, Tammy felt bad about invading the privacy of others. And so she only did it sometimes. Maybe just a few of mother's memories here and there. Maybe just a few of Kingsley's—she loved Kingsley's memories the best—and then some of Allison's. Mary Lou, her aunt, had *boring* memories. The "reliving the memories" part was strange and exciting, and at first, Tammy hadn't known what to make of it. In the beginning, she would find herself in the middle of the memory and be confused. Later, she learned to follow the trail of the memory to the beginning. After that, she learned to move "through the memory," which was the only way she knew how to think about it. She saw herself as a spirit, moving forward within the memory. Memories, after all, were really just long comic strips, so to speak. She could touch down at any point and sort of hit the play button.

Her mother could do something similar, but it took her more effort. Tammy, on the other hand, could lie in bed and do a number of things at once—and one of them was to relive memories even as she was doing homework. If, say, Mom was having wine with Mary Lou in the living room, Tammy needed only to dip into her aunt's mind, and idly poke around for the highlighted memories. Her boring memories! Except for a few wild years in college, her aunt was one big bore-fest.

Anyway, the fun thing about memories was that there were always more of them. Each day, each hour created new ones, and Tammy scanned them

J.R. RAIN

all, continuously and often. Yes, she knew she had a problem, but she also sort of saw herself as a kind of guardian, too. No one, but no one, was coming to this house without her knowing what kind of person they were.

Her father had lucked out in the sense that he had died *before* Tammy's gifts had fully matured. In a way, she was glad her father had died before she could dip into his mind. Quite honestly, she was afraid of what she might have found there.

The problem was... now she was getting snatches of her father's mind within Anthony's mind. Snatches that filtered through her brother's thoughts—a mind she rarely, if ever, dipped into. Her brother's seriously *gross* mind.

After all, Tammy was certain that her brother had crushes on every female at his school, including some of their more curvy teachers. And not just crushes... but fantasies.

She shuddered. *So, so gross.*

The problem was—and this was why Tammy was currently *not* dating—her brother was not very different than all the boys at her school. Like *all* the boys. In fact, compared to some, her brother was tame!

Tammy was turned off—no repelled—by the young males of her species. She literally wanted nothing to do with them. Certainly not now, and maybe not for a long time, if ever.

Tammy had gotten quite good at letting feelings

70

"slip away," as she called it. She had to. She saw too much, relived too much, heard too much, knew too much. She recognized early on the need to let go of the unwanted thoughts. Only the very good ones were permitted to stay. After all, some memories were just too juicy to let go of!

And her mom was full of them. Just packed with them. The good news was, Tammy had probed her mother's mind so much that she now knew which memories to avoid completely. These were the highlighted and slightly pulsating memories. Such memories were bound to traumatize Tammy for days. Yes, these were the memories of her mother and Kingsley... being intimate. Which she avoided like the plague.

Besides the gross memories, her mother was full of so many... wonderful and fantastic memories. In fact, just a few months ago, her mother had had the most amazing conversation with Dracula. Freakin' Dracula! And Tammy loved the memories of her mother flying as the giant dragon, Talos.

Cool stuff was always happening to her mom, and now tonight was the biggest whammy of them all.

Tammy was like 99% certain her mom had had a conversation with God.

But that wasn't even the half of it.

The memories of heaven that Tammy had relived in her mother's mind were like nothing she had ever seen before. Like nothing *anyone* had ever seen before. It was a heaven that most people were destined for, even those who went to hell and had their hell experience. Yes, Tammy had also relived her mother's conversation with the devil himself, and knew that hell wasn't really real. Not the way people thought of it. Oh, sure it was as real as people allowed it to be—the same with the devil, who had been created out of the ether to fulfill a role. He was literally thought turned into creation by mass expectation. Tammy was pretty sure she understood this.

She folded her hands behind her head and smiled.

The devil and God all within three months.

Wow, Mom!

Tammy had reviewed all the conversations her mom had had with the Librarian—or the Alchemist, as her mom sometimes referred to Archibald Maximus, the cute guy who oversaw the secret occult reading room at Cal State Fullerton, and who also helped run a school for Light Warriors, of which Tammy may or may not be one of. She didn't think she was, but there was always that possibility. The school took in kids her age, though usually younger than her—and trained them to fight the dark masters who sought to re-enter the world. Creepy stuff, all of it. She had yet to meet Maximus, and had yet to probe his mind. She suspected many secrets to the universe would await if she did so. He was, after all, a human who had found immortality. He didn't have to drink all that nasty blood or host a dark master through some nefarious dark magicks that involved tainted blood, like her mom and Kingsley and Dracula and Fang had to go through. Like Allison, the Alchemist's blood was clean. Unlike Allison, he was immortal.

Tammy idly wondered if Allison had any new fun memories. Her last batch of them had been crazy as hell, and involved the world's creepiest hunting lodge in Oregon. So, so creepy. But Tammy loved the memory, and loved watching how Allison and her triad of witches had overcome something very wicked indeed.

But heaven?

Holy sweet mama—it had been so beautiful! It had also been a lot to take in, even for her mother who had witnessed it firsthand. Her mother, who had been crying through it all, all while being led by the hand of God himself, a short man who just might also be a homeless man, too. Tammy wasn't sure, although her mother did have a vague memory of meeting the man at a Denny's years ago.

She met God... *twice!!*

Tammy was almost developing a newfound respect for her mother. Almost. Her mother was, of course, still her mother, and thus a dork. Like a royal dork. Her mother's fashion was at least two years out of date. And her make-up was almost always a little off. Too much foundation here. Too much mascara there. Tammy knew her mother wore the make-up so that when her picture was randomly taken at any number of places—or security cameras the world over—her mother would, you know, actually *show up* in the picture, and not look like the invisible woman with animated high-cut mom jeans and sneakers that no one, but no one, wore anymore.

Such a dork.

But Tammy felt sorry for her mother, too.

She thought about her mother's conversation with God, and knew all over again that the heaven her mother had been shown was not meant for her—or any vampire, or werewolf, or Lichtenstein monster. While the dark masters who shared their bodies, and thus robbed them of heaven, fled back to wherever the hell they hid from the devil, the original host—her mom, for instance—would be reabsorbed back into the Source of all Life.

Back into God.

There was no heaven for Mom, and that made Tammy feel terrible. But didn't God say something about heaven being here, on earth, for her mother? He had. He had told her to look for the good here, to see the good here, and she would catch a glimpse of heaven, every day. In effect, as long as her mother lived, earth *was* her heaven. And if mankind ever reached the stars, the stars would be her heaven, too. She wouldn't have to be reabsorbed back into God, whatever the hell that meant.

Tammy was not surprised to find the tears on

her cheeks as she lay there in the dark, thinking of her mother dying, and becoming one once again with God; of her mother never, ever seeing that beautiful place called heaven.

So beautiful, thought Tammy.

She clenched her fist and decided right then and there that, dork or not, she would do all she could for the rest of her life to keep her mother alive, if possible. The problem was, her mother was, like, always putting herself in the world's most dangerous situations to help others. It was like her mother was asking for it. Asking to die.

No, thought Tammy. She wasn't asking to die. Not ever. She was looking to help people—pretty much anyone who came to her, her mother would help them. Well, usually for a little money, of course—unless the client had none, and then her mom would do it for free. Free! Who did that these days?

Her mom did. That's who. Her mom who sacrificed her own eternity to help others.

That put another lump in Tammy's throat and she fought it, but lost and found herself weeping again.

She was just drying her eyes when she heard her mother approaching. She could hear her footsteps— and her thoughts. Her thoughts were... interesting. It appeared her mother, who had been reading a manuscript all evening long, was sort of lost in this fantasy world. Although Tammy hadn't read the book, she saw the vivid images in her mother's mind as she relived her favorite scenes—and replayed her favorite snatches of dialogue. From what Tammy could tell, this was a damn good book. It also felt *real* to her, and real to her mother in particular. So real that she knew her mother was currently struggling with a rather audacious concept. (Tammy was certain she'd used the word audacious correctly.) The concept centered around a woman in the story—the heroine—a woman with whom her mother had come to love the way all bibliophiles came to love their favorite characters. Tammy saw the woman plain as day in her mother's thoughts. The thing was... this was a woman forged from her mother's imagination, cobbled together from the words of the book. Except...

Except this woman looked so real, so very real.

This confused her mother, too.

And Tammy saw why. Boy, did she see why.

Mommy's gonna be busy tonight, she thought. She also knew her mother had secretly emailed the book to herself, without telling her client. And, further, that she had emailed the book to Allison, as well. Her mother was such a sneak.

Speaking of whom, her mother paused just outside her door. Tammy could sense her mother collecting her thoughts before pushing aside her thoughts to give herself fully to her daughter. Tammy liked that about her mom, who always gave Tammy her full attention. And when her bedroom door cracked open, she knew what her mother was going to say before she said it.

"I'm—"

"Heading out. I know, Mom."

Silhouetted in the light of the door, she saw her mother's head dip, noting her mom's hair was slightly askew. She knew her mother couldn't even see her own hair—part of the curse of that devil woman inside her. Tammy surprised herself by swinging her legs out of bed and hurrying over to her mother and throwing her arms around her.

"Be careful tonight, okay?"

Her mother blinked at that, then nodded, and smiled. "Of course, sweetie. You okay? Have you been crying?"

"It's nothing—"

"You want to talk?"

"No, no. You need to get to that guy's house before midnight. The ghost and all."

"You know about that, huh?" asked her mom.

"I know about a lot."

"What else do you know about the ghost?"

"I know she's not a ghost."

Her mother nodded. "Yeah, I'm thinking that maybe she's not either."

Her mother smiled at that, but then the smile wavered, and Tammy knew her mother was thinking about what she'd seen today: her vision of paradise. Tammy wondered if catching a glimpse of heaven was worse than never experiencing it. Her mother said, "Not much escapes you, huh?"

"No, Mom." Tammy paused and then reached out and fixed her mom's hair. The jeans and sneakers were beyond fixing, but there was at least hope for her hair.

"Better?" her mom asked.

"A lot better. But you're still a dork."

"That goes without saying. You are to stay here, with your brother."

"You mean the Fire Warrior who can, like, kick seven or eight werewolves' asses all by himself? Him?"

"Yeah, him. Keep an eye on him, and an ear."

"A telepathic ear?"

"Yes. I'm worried about him."

Tammy nodded and watched her mom move back through the hallway and open her brother's door to let him know she was leaving. Tammy knew that her brother was in the middle of an internal conversation with their dad, a man who turned out to be a royal sleaze, for which Tammy wasn't sure she could ever forgive him.

When her mother was gone, Tammy went back to her bed and lay there, and relived heaven all over again.

Again and again...

12.

I had a lot on my mind.

Enough that I was certain I had gone through three of four red lights with nary a memory of passing through them. And was nary even a word? It was, I was certain of it. Okay, ninety percent certain. Maybe eighty.

Anyway, it wasn't often one met God. Then again, I had met him twice, hadn't I?

I had.

I think.

The homeless man on the street, yes, after much thought, I was certain I had seen him before, at a Denny's years ago. A homeless man who had known everything about me. And I mean, *everything*.

God, certainly.

Then again, from what I could tell of my vision of heaven, God was in all things. In heaven, everything pulsed with light. God's light. And everything was connected. The light touched everything and was everything, wove through everything, pulsated with everything, and I knew now that light was God. Or whatever you wanted to call him. Or her. Of course, the person I had met today was a man. But it could have just as easily been a woman. Or a floating ball of light. Or a voice from the sky. From what I understood, he appeared as we expected him to appear, which apparently made it easier for all involved.

The devil, I knew, *possessed* his followers.

God probably did the same. Or not. If you were the creator of all that is and will forever be, conjuring up a temporary flesh and blood body wouldn't be much of a big deal. Besides, I was fairly certain angels did just that.

But not demons. They were bodiless, I knew.

Until they possessed a willing human. Or *mostly* willing. Or the cursed.

The nature of God was a heady subject, and I had been given a glimpse of his magnificence. Then again, wasn't the earth around me a glimpse of it as well? It was, and it was more than a glimpse.

You can make heaven on Earth, Sam. Now, in this place.

I thought about that as I drove steadily on into the night, toward a home with a ghost that wasn't a ghost. I was pretty sure of that.

And so was Tammy. My freakishly powerful daughter who knew way too much.

No. Was *exposed* to way too much.

Except, of course, there was nothing I could do about that.

Although that might not be true.

I suspected *space* might lessen her power. As in giving her some. When I was in New Orleans, my daughter let it be known that her telepathic powers had wavered somewhat. At the least, they had not expanded. My very *proximity* gave her power, and that was a difficult concept to wrap my mind around. The further—and longer—I was away from my daughter, the more normal she would be.

I thought about that as I drove through another intersection.

God, I hoped the light was green.

My phone rang. My old minivan didn't have Bluetooth capability. Luckily, I happen to be quicker than everyone else and so I wasn't too concerned with safety when I snatched up my phone. Also, I had a little something called an *inner alarm*, which was kind of like auto braking but way cooler. It was Allison calling.

"Talk to me," I said.

"Most people say hello."

"Most people don't have an Allison in their lives."

"What's that supposed to mean?"

81

"That you're so pretty?"

"Honestly, I don't know why I try, Sam."

"Because you love me."

"Just be nice to me, okay? I'm like the only real friend you have."

I thought about that. I certainly had other friends, but it was true: Allison was the only real friend I had who was there for me through hell or high water, and who really wanted nothing from me. Except my time. And attention. And love. Hmm.

"Maybe," I said.

"There's no maybe about it. I'm your best friend, so deal with it."

"Bitch," I said.

"No," she said. "Witch."

I laughed and asked her why she was bothering me.

"Bothering you? Sam—"

"Just get on with it."

"Fine," she said. "I just finished reading Charlie Reed's book. Or his unfinished book."

"What do you think?"

"What do I think? What do I think?? My God, I think I haven't truly lived until now. That story, those characters. I mean, I only just stopped crying a few minutes ago."

I knew what she meant. "Pretty good, huh?"

"Pretty good? It was transcendent. It was life-changing."

It would have been easy to say she was overreacting. Except I knew she wasn't. In between my thoughts of God, heaven, my kids and Danny... I found myself back in the book. Back into Charlie's carefully and perfectly realized world. Back with his characters. Back with their problems and loves and hopes and dreams. Back with Queen Autumn and her search for her kidnapped daughter.

"Sam, will he be finishing the book anytime soon?"

"I have no idea."

"I kinda need to know what's going to happen."

"I kinda need to know, too."

"Sam, there's something else."

"The ghost," I said, without needing to read her mind, even if I could.

"Yes, Sam. Of course, I haven't seen the ghost personally, but I saw her there in your memory, and she's..."

"Queen Autumn," I said.

"Yes," said Allison. "I think she is."

"You do understand how crazy we sound."

"Said the vampire to the witch."

"Everything we do and say from here until eternity will sound crazy," I said, nodding. I kept my phone in my lap, with Allison on speaker. As in most states, California prohibits drivers from using handheld wireless phones. I often wondered where balancing a cell phone on your knee fell into that category. Either way, I could probably telepathically convince a cop to not give me a ticket, but who likes getting pulled over in the first place? Better to keep the phone on speaker and out of eyesight, and hope to someday afford a newer van.

Of course, I heard a distant voice speaking as if from a deep well, reminding me that I didn't *have* to wait for anything, that I could take what I wanted, and compel others to give me what I wanted. I told that voice to go to hell.

"Did you just tell me to go to hell?" asked Allison.

"No, sorry."

"Elizabeth?"

"Yes," I said. "And if you can hear my thoughts, then you must be close by."

"Look to your right."

I did, and there was Allison in the lane next to me, hunched over her steering wheel like a sea captain in a nor'easter.

"I heard that," she said. "I'm what you call a *close driver*."

"Did you just make that up?" I asked.

"I did," she said, her voice reaching me through the phone a fraction after her lips had moved. The miracles of science. She shot me a quick, furtive glance. Allison was also what you called a *nervous driver*. I noted the Bluetooth in her ear. "So what are we going to do about Autumn?" she asked.

"We figure out what she wants."

"But she's from the realm of Dur and speaks

Durian," said Allison.

"We need help," I said. "Serious help."

"Maybe Charlie knows how—"

"Not that kind of help," I snapped, and clicked off.

After all, we had arrived.

13.

The three of us were in Charlie's study. So far, there was no sign of the ghost. Or Autumn. Or whoever or whatever she was. Then again, it was only 11:30 p.m.

"And you're telling me the woman in my story—a book I have yet to finish or publish, and have barely let out of my sight—is our ghost?"

"We think so, yes."

"And you've read the book, too?" he said to Allison.

"I did, yes. It's very good. I can't wait to see how it all turns—"

He whipped his head around to me. "And how did you get the book?"

"You emailed it to me."

"I don't remember doing that. I've been so

closely guarding it. I mean, I remember letting you read it here, but..."

I telepathically eased his mind, told him this was a non-issue and that he was okay with it, because Allison and I were super-special, awesome girls, and he was more than okay sharing his book with us.

"Boy, I'm relieved you like it! You know, you're the only two people to even read it."

"I feel honored," said Allison.

"And I can breathe easier. You just never know if these things are any good."

"Is this your first book?" asked Allison.

"It is."

"How old are you, if you don't mind me asking?"

"Forty-four."

"Why did you wait so long to write your first book?"

Allison and I were sitting on the sofa. Charlie had pulled around his desk chair. Allison sat maybe a little closer than I was comfortable with. She *harrumphed* at that, and moved over.

"Rude," she whispered.

"What can I say?" I whispered back. "I'm not a close sitter."

"Excuse me?" said Charlie.

"Sorry," said Allison. "My friend here is a prima donna."

Charlie smiled and sat back and nodded as if he

cared, but he didn't. Minor as it was, he and I now had a mindlink, and I could sense him turning her question over and over in his mind. Finally, he said, "I wasn't ready, I guess. I didn't feel like I knew the characters enough. I... and this is going to sound strange... I wanted to, well..."

We waited. Charlie shifted uncomfortably.

"I'll just say it," he said, turning a shade of red. "I wanted to, well, love them first."

"Love them?" asked Allison.

"Yes," he said.

"And do you love them now?"

"More than you know."

"I think we know, Charlie," I said. "It kinda comes across in the story."

"Oh, thank God," he said. "I mean, I knew I loved them, but I wasn't sure if I was able to *convey* that to the reader."

"You conveyed the crap out of it," said Allison.

I nearly added my own praise but figured Allison had blown enough sunshine up his ass. I knew Charlie hadn't recognized his "ghost" because he hadn't actually seen her. I had seen her, using the second sight that I had been blessed—or cursed—with. The sight that sees the energetic world side by side with the physical.

Charlie might have caught a snatch of this thought, because he asked, "How can you two be so sure the ghost is Autumn? I mean, no offense, but you weren't even here when Sam saw the ghost—"

"Oh, she described it in great detail," said Allison. "Sam has an amazing flair for details. It's what makes her such a great detective. And why she thinks so highly of herself. And why, possibly, she takes her friends for granted."

"Um..." said Charlie.

Allie, cool it, I thought, knowing she could read my thoughts, even if hers were presently blocked from me. At the same time, I instructed Charlie to forget what he was about to hear in the next few minutes.

I turned to Allison. "Whatever I said to you, I'm sorry."

"You say lots of mean things, Sam. Things that make me feel small. I'm not small. I'm just as powerful as you, in my own right. You should see the things I can do now."

"I have seen them, and you are powerful, and you are not small. Look, can we have this talk later?"

"Why not now? In fact, I insist we talk about it now—there you go again!"

"What?" Except I suspected I knew what.

"Damn straight you know what. You rolled your eyes. Again. As in, what I think and want isn't as important as what you think and want."

"I didn't say that."

"But your eyes said it!"

"I can't help what my eyes do."

"Yes, you can, Sam. Just like you can help what

you say and think."

"Thinking is trickier. And if you look deep enough, you will see I have nothing but respect and..." I hesitated. It was a natural instinct not to give Allison too much. When I gave her an inch, she took a mile.

"What, Sam? I want to hear it. Or do you have that word permanently blocked from me?"

"It's not permanently blocked. You know I do. We've been through a lot together."

"Then say it, Sam. Say it in front of Charlie too."

"Charlie's not listening to us," I said. "Not really."

"Well, say it anyway."

"Do I have to?"

"Yes."

"You shouldn't make someone say it. It should come out naturally."

"Well, naturally for you is like pulling teeth."

"I'm not sure that metaphor makes sense—"

"Say it, damn it."

"Fine," I said. "I respect and like you."

"Sam..."

"I respect and adore you?"

"Sam, you suck."

"You can't make someone say I love you," I said. "Even friends."

"Well, it doesn't seem like you do sometimes."

"You know I do, Allie. You can see it right

there in my thoughts."

She knew I did, and she obviously saw it there in my thoughts.

"You really do, Sam?"

"Of course, now can we get back to—"

She threw herself on me, hugging me far too hard, and getting way, way up in my personal space. "I love you, too, Sam! More than you know."

"I know," I said, rolling the crap out of my eyes. "I know."

"I see that, Sam. There's a mirror behind you."

"Liar," I said. Yes, I had enough make up on to *mostly* show up in mirrors, but not my eyeballs. Never my eyeballs.

"Fine. I lied. But I don't care. And yes, that was you giving an inch, and this is me taking a mile. Deal with it. And have you ever considered colored contacts?"

***

"I'm sorry, I seem to have lost my train of thought," said Charlie. "What were we talking about?"

"We were talking about how the ghost might just be Queen Autumn from your unfinished novel," I said.

"Right." He shook his head a little. "And what makes you think the ghost is a character from my novel?"

"We don't for sure. But we think it might be one and the same."

"But a ghost is a ghost... and a character is, well, made up." He tapped his brain. "In here."

"That, admittedly, is the tricky part."

Charlie stood and seemed to regain the confidence he'd displayed the other day, when he hired me. "I mean, I would never have believed in ghosts either. But these past few months... it's undeniable. Just undeniable. Something is here." I saw in his mind's eye again the fleeting glimpses he had of movement. Glimpses only. No details. I saw again the flickering blue light, the mist, the sense of being watched. All of this played out in his mind, and all of it was, admittedly, strong indicators of a *typical* haunting. "And you, Sam? You believe it's her?"

"I do," I said, "and I think it's time that I show you what I saw."

"Show me? Wait. What?"

"Sit next to me, Charlie," I said.

He was pacing, but paused and sat between Allison and I. He shivered a little when his forearm brushed my own arm. I tried not to be offended.

"Close your eyes," I said.

"Why—"

"It'll be okay," I said, adding a small suggestion that all would be okay, and his eyes promptly closed.

I didn't want him too deep, because I wanted him to remember what he was seeing, so I gave him a series of prompts to remember the image I was about to convey to him, and to also believe that I had *drawn* the image for him. And when he was calm and receptive, I gave him a clear view, telepathically, of the woman in my own memory, and he gasped.

And then he wept.

14.

"Can I keep this?" he asked, reaching for the closest piece of paper, a bill from AT&T. Yes, he believed this was my drawing of Autumn.

"Sure," I said, and reinforced the belief that the image he saw in his mind's eye—the image I had transferred to him—was, in fact, clearly displayed on the phone bill before him. Briefly, I saw what he saw: a surprisingly lifelike portrait of Autumn smiling back at him.

"Her eyes look so real," he said, staring closely at his phone bill. "You really are a wonderful artist, Samantha. I mean, this is *exactly* how I imagined her." He held up the page for Allison to see, showing her the AT&T logo and columns of numbers.

"She's a regular Picasso," said Allison drily.

As Charlie stared at his phone bill, often

reaching out and brushing it lightly with his finger-tips, Allison motioned with her head for me to follow her, which I did into the very hallway where I'd seen the full-body apparition of Queen Autumn.

Allison, privy to my thoughts, scanned the area. "There's no ghost here. In fact, I don't *feel* a ghost anywhere in this house."

My psychic, witchy friend was almost as good at perceiving ghosts as I was. Almost. She didn't quite see the world of energy and light that I did. Nor did she see the minor and often fleeting manifestations, or the ever-flowing currents of well-being. She didn't see, for instance, the briefest hint of a dog manifesting in the far corner of the hallway, then disappear again. But she did catch it in my thoughts.

She turned and looked in the corner. "Really, a dog?"

"It came and went, so fleeting as almost to not be here."

"A ghost dog?"

"Almost, but not quite. The wavering hint of a *memory* of a dog."

"But how?" she asked.

"Its imprint could be stamped upon this place, or it was just swinging by to say hello. Then again, it might have realized it had the wrong house. It was just a dog, after all."

"Do you see her now?" asked Allison. "Autumn?"

"She's not here, but this hallway..." I let my voice trail off and frowned. I hadn't really looked at the hallway before. Or, rather, I hadn't looked too deeply. "This hallway is particularly lively."

Allison saw what I was seeing in my mind's eye, so tuned in was she to me.

"You are seeing mini-manifestations everywhere, Sam. They're coming and going rapidly."

And so I was. I turned in the hallway, tuning into the energy, and watching the various eddying pools of flowing light coagulate into faces and shapes and blobs, only to disperse again. I looked toward the end of the long hallway, where the light was flowing through walls and passing through us. Some of this wasn't new to me. All light behaved this way. Although I had come to know it not as light, but as a never-ending flow of well-being, the energy that creates worlds. I always suspected that those who harnessed the energy, through focused thought and right action, had the best results. It was energy available to all. I just happened to see it, and it lit my way, even in the darkest of rooms.

But this hallway had one difference: the sheer amount of manifestations.

"What does it mean, Sam?" asked Allison, who had been following my train of thought.

"I don't know."

She nodded, frowned. "It's like we're standing in a tunnel of creation."

"Why tunnel?" I asked.

"It sounds more mysterious."

"Oh, brother," I said.

She snapped her head around because she had caught in my mind's eye the merest hint of a stag or horse manifesting behind her, and charging at her. She shuddered as it went through her. "Sam, what's going on here? Have you seen something like this before?"

"No, not really. Not that I can recall. I mean, some areas tend to have a lot of spirit activity. Cemeteries. Hospitals. Old homes. Busy street corners."

"Where people have died in accidents?"

"Yes," I said.

"But you aren't seeing much human activity," she said. "I mean, I can see some manifestations that *could* be human. But many more are animal shapes. Some tiny and some quite—whoa!"

Something swooped down the hallway, over our heads, something that flapped with great wings, only to disappear through the far wall. Allison, had she not been seeing through my own inner eye, would have missed it.

"I wish I had missed it, Sam."

"No, you don't."

She nodded. "No, I don't. This is so fascinating and kind of scary. That was no bird. It was..."

"A dragon," I said.

"The ghost of a dragon?"

I paused. "I didn't get a sense it was a ghost."

"It felt real, huh, Sam? Like it was just passing through."

My friend, I think, was right.

"What's happening, Sam?"

"I don't know," I said. "But let's get back to loverboy before he runs off to Vegas and marries his phone bill."

***

The night was uneventful.

Queen Autumn didn't make another appearance, although Charlie's side hallway was a veritable superhighway of creation. Animals swept across the arched opening, and from where we sat in the office, Allison and I could see deer and rabbits and wolves and, once, long processions of people—all of which came and went quickly, flowing down the hallway, wavering in and out of existence. It was, quite frankly, the ultimate light show.

All the while, Charlie stared down at his AT&T phone bill, lovingly touching it and stroking it like a star-crossed lover.

15.

I left my minivan parked in front of Charlie's home, disrobed on his bedroom balcony under the dark of night, and, with Allison on her way home and Charlie snoozing—thanks to a suggestion of mine—I launched myself out as far and wide as possible.

Now, as his pool came rushing at me, something else rushed at me, too. Something beastly, and located directly in the center of the single flame. A flame that I had conjured. A flame that I had come to know as a portal between worlds—and a portal between time and space, too. If not time, then definitely space.

Now I felt myself rushing toward the creature in the flame. Except, of course, I wasn't rushing. I was still falling toward the covered pool.

But that's exactly what it felt like: *rushing*, movement forward, the sense of two creatures meeting somewhere in the middle. The middle of where, I didn't know, but suddenly I wasn't falling anymore. No, not at all. I was gliding, with great outstretched arms that manipulated the air. Now, I was riding a cushion of air up and over the brick wall that separated Charlie's house from his neighbor's. I flapped once, twice, and now I was rocketing up, higher and higher.

And higher.

Hi Talos, I thought.

Hello Sam, came the voice in my head. A deep voice, with melodic overtones. A gentle and wise voice, too. I knew that in Talos's world, communication was done primarily through telepathy, but I had a question.

Do you have a voice, Talos?

I have no need for a voice, Sam.

If you were to open your mouth and speak?

It would sound as a great roar.

Then why does your "voice" sound deep to me? Why wouldn't it sound, I dunno, neutral?

I leveled off at a free-flowing air current that I knew to be a jet stream. Had I chosen to ride it to Hawaii, I could have. I knew Talos was capable of reaching great speeds, too. No doubt I would be there before sunrise. Then what? I couldn't afford a hotel room out there.

The internal voice is nearly as real as the

physical, Sam.

So someone could have a high or deep internal voice?

Of course.

At present, Talos's wings were outstretched and flapping just enough to keep me level—us level, since I was pretty sure I was the one doing the flying.

Indeed, Sam. We've talked about this.

But isn't it a little like giving the keys to a dopey teenager?

You're hardly dopey.

But I'd never flown before.

No, but you were a quick learner. Nearly expert now.

Nearly?

Oh, there are some things I can do that you haven't tried.

I haven't pushed you to your limits yet, you're saying.

Something like that.

I could only shake my head. Hell, I'd taken him deep beneath the ocean, and all the way out into space, the moon and Mars, respectively. What else could the big fella do?

You need only ask, Sam.

Okay, maybe I will. Someday.

I'm always here, Sam.

I know, I thought. *I mean, I think I know. Tell me again how we connected, Talos? Tell me how you found me, or I found you?*

The answer is multifaceted and far-reaching, Sam.

I have all the time in the world.

My world and your world are deeply connected, as evidenced by the dragons in your mythology, both past and present.

I'm following so far.

We have a keen interest in your world, which is not very different from our own.

Except yours is much more highly evolved.

Much, much more.

Okay, no need to rub it in.

No rubbing, Sam. We are many millions of years ahead of you.

That's a lot of evolving going on, I thought.

Precisely. And your highly evolved dark masters reached out to us.

How did they find you?

The worlds are not as separated as you might think, Sam. Indeed, you and I are only a flame away. But in their case, before a connection was made with us, they used astral traveling.

Conscious sleep? I asked.

Close, Sam. Meditation would be a better word. Many on your planet do it. But not all travel to new worlds.

And you formed a friendship with them?

Not quite. We saw an opportunity.

You do understand they are called dark masters

for a reason? I asked.

We knew their nature, Sam.

What did they want from you?

A partnership, of sorts. They sought to use us in their wars.

And you agreed?

We do not fight wars, Sam.

I thought about that. I also thought about the few times I had summoned Talos to fight my own wars.

I used you to kill, I thought.

Indeed.

And you are okay with that?

I give myself to you, Sam, for you to use as you see fit.

Would you prefer I didn't use you to kill?

I trust you are making the best choices for you and those you love.

I flapped his great wings. The process seemed effortless, but I could feel the great force behind each downthrust, a blast of wind that, I imagined, raced all the way to the land far below. Somewhere down there a man's toupee had just blown off. That gave me a giggle.

That's a lot of trust, I finally thought.

The trust goes both ways, Sam.

I nodded at that. *My body is with you, in your world.*

Safe and sound.

Am I in my body? I asked. *I mean, am I holding*

a conversation with you there?

No, Sam. You are sitting next to me, quietly, waiting.

Because I have not mastered the art to being in two places at the same time.

Not yet. No.

But maybe someday?

Maybe, Sam. If it serves a purpose for you.

I considered the full extent of his words. *So the dark masters thought they were using you, but, in fact, you were using them?*

That is safe to say.

And how, exactly, are you using them?

By finding our way to you. And others like you.

Other vampires?

Yes, Sam.

For what purpose?

To help and guide and to spread the truth of what they are. To show them another way. To remind them that they are much more than the entity within.

Thank you, Talos. And thank the others.

I sensed him nodding in my mind.

I asked, *How many vampires can presently summon creatures like you?*

Perhaps a half dozen.

Wow. I feel honored.

You should.

But how did we—you and I—link up, so to speak? How did you know to find me? How did I find you? How did you know to come to me on that night, five years ago, when I jumped out of the hotel balcony?

You could say we have a special bond, Sam.

How special?

We will save that for another time, and I will answer your question then.

I'm holding you to it.

He laughed lightly, although I sensed a lot of emotion behind his words, which confused and fascinated me.

We were silent for a long time, when I asked, *Talos, should Elizabeth take over me completely, could she still summon you?*

Yes.

And control you?

Yes.

But I thought you said she gets ejected each time I connect with you. That this is our safe place. But before he could answer, the answer came to me. *Never mind. I think I know. I would be the one who is ejected, then.*

Indeed, Sam.

And Dracula? I know he, too, can transform into his own dragon.

The man you call Dracula is doing his best to fight the entity within him.

But he's mostly losing, I thought.

He is in, it is safe to say, the fight of his life.

We were silent, even as the wind thundered over

Talos's ears. That is, if he even had ears. I twitched... *something*. I think it was an ear.

I have ears, Sam.

Good to know.

I continued flapping, each movement slow and methodical, effortless yet powerful. I sensed this was Talos's optimum speed. His *trot* so to speak. His natural gait. I also sensed that Talos could fly like this from now until eternity.

Not quite that long, Sam. But put it this way: we could see much of your world before I needed rest.

What about eating?

I do not eat, Sam.

This was news to me. I had always assumed the big fellow partook in a fat cow or two, at least every now and then.

Maybe back in the day, Sam. But not anymore.

I frowned at this. Or tried to frown. For all I knew, Talos's face did nothing at all.

So what do you do for nourishment? Pardon me for pointing out the obvious, but you are a big son-of-a-bitch. And with all of this flying and spouting fire, well, I can only imagine the calories you burn through. No pun intended.

I heard a light flicker of laughter in my head. *All good points, Sam. But those of my kind consume universal energy.*

Say again.

Universal energy. A life source that is available to all, continuously.

Not quite all, I thought.

Not true, Sam. There are those on your earth who do not eat—at least, not in the traditional sense. These are what you would call a master's master.

Um, what is this universal energy? Where is it?

It is everywhere, Sam.

Are you eating now? Did I just consume a universal cheeseburger and not know it?

More chuckling. *In a way, yes. Those who are open to it are satiated continuously.*

So you are never hungry?

Never.

And your belly is full or empty?

My belly, for the most part, has been shut down.

Because you have no use for it.

Something like that.

And how often do you eat?

Continuously.

What does universal energy taste like?

There is no taste, Sam. There is only a sense of contentment, of nourishment, of strength.

Do I have access to this now? I thought.

Now? There was a long pause. A really long pause. *I do not know, Sam. It is for you to decide.*

I thought about this. I also thought about never drinking blood again. And I was intrigued. I asked: *What, exactly, is it?*

It is best described as a source of well-being that permeates everything.

Is it God?

It is from God. From the creator. You have heard this before. This is not new information to you, Sam.

I did not know this well-being could also, you know, be a midnight snack too.

Like your kind says: you learn something new every day.

I thought about this in silence, flapping Talos's great wings, and soaring high over Southern California and its glittering, rolling hills.

16.

"You have a question, Sam," said the young man who wasn't so young after we'd greeted. Archibald Maximus, the Occult Reading Room Librarian, or guardian, depending on who showed up.

"I do, yes. And you don't say hello anymore?"

"Hello, Sam. My apologies. I was busy back... there." He gestured vaguely behind him, toward a short hallway with a number of doors leading off to either side, a hallway I'd never been down—or had even been invited down.

He'd hinted what was back there. Doorways to elsewhere, even doorways to the magical school where he taught. Once, he even hinted that his lab was back there, too.

A somewhat random thought occurred to me.

"You're not a teacher, are you? You run the school."

"I'm the headmaster, yes."

"Like Dumbledore," I said.

He smiled at me. "Maybe. Little does J.K. Rowling know just how much she drew from the real world."

"Is she a channel?"

"Yes, but more. A lot more."

I nodded as if I knew what the hell he meant. I said, "Why aren't you headmastering now? Okay, that sounded bad. But you know what I meant. Why aren't you at school?"

"Because I am here, Sam."

"But you are not here all the time. Only a few hours of the day. And surely you aren't here when there is no need to be."

"I come when summoned."

"The doors behind you." I counted eight of them. "Are doorways to other places, correct?"

"Portals, correct."

"You can pop in here whenever you need to, and then pop back out to the school, or somewhere else."

He nodded once. "Some of the doors lead to even more doors, Sam."

"You be-bop around the country."

He raised his eyes a little, waited.

"You be-bop around the world?"

He waited.

I swallowed. "Other worlds?"

"A handful of worlds. But there are still more to explore."

"Am I really having this conversation?"

"You are."

"What am I taking you away from, presently? I mean, prior to coming here, what were you doing?"

"I was inspecting the security of the school. Making my rounds, so to speak."

"You really are Dumbledore," I said. "But younger. And cuter."

"Are you trying to make me blush, Sam?"

Except he hadn't blushed, I noted. For all his cuteness and youth, the Alchemist was a bit of an enigma. He was, in essence, an immortal by choice. An immortal without the aid of a highly evolved dark master.

"I never said that, Sam," he said. "You assumed this."

I blinked. Outside, through the opaque glass window, I watched a student sashay by, her ponytail swinging back and forth, her backpack looking far lighter than any of mine ever had. I supposed many textbooks these days were available on Kindle.

I said, after processing his words, "You've been entrusted with a school to train Light Warriors. You watch over the world's most dangerous books. You fight the good fight. There's no way a highly evolved dark master is inside—" I stopped short.

He looked at me, waited again.

"It's not a dark master," I said.

He raised his eyebrows.

I nodded. "It's an angel."

"Very good, Sam. But I am not possessed. It is a mutual joining, if you will. He comes and goes as he sees fit, especially when I summon him."

"Is the angel with you now?" I asked.

"Yes."

"But why?"

"I find his presence... comforting."

I got his meaning. "You mean, comforting when you are meeting me?"

Archibald Maximus opened his mouth to speak, then closed it again. It was, I think, the first time he had ever been at a loss for words. He tried again. "Sam, you are not like the other vampires."

"Because...?"

"My mother, for one thing. And she herself is not like other dark masters, either. She was particularly gifted in the dark arts, and particularly... evil. Worse, she was manipulative and vengeful. Combine her temperament and abilities with your own inherent witchy talents—"

"I never developed my witchy talents, not in this life, not yet, anyway—"

"No, but they are there, dormant."

"But I thought I lost my ability to perform witchcraft once I became a vampire."

"No, Sam. You only lost your place within the triad of your sisters."

"I can still practice witchcraft?"

"Oh, yes. You will find it comes easy to you, much as it did with Allison."

Witchcraft? I'd never thought... I'd never dreamed...

"You met someone yesterday," he said suddenly.

I blinked, snapped out of it. "I did, kind of. We shared a pen, you could say."

"Oh, you shared more than that. He shared something with you that is new information to me, too. I'm sorry if I am prying, but I can see it there, in your memory, plain as day."

I knew of that which he spoke. I waited.

"I will admit," he said, "that it never occurred to me that some of the vampires' talents come from their very souls expressing themselves."

"Like a big-ass dragon just told me, you learn something new every day."

He was nodding. "This is huge, Sam." The Librarian was pacing behind the help desk. I suppose I could also call him 'Headmaster' too. A man of many titles. "It means we have been giving the dark masters far too much credit. Note how they never corrected us. Note that they wanted us to believe in their power. But in fact, it was and is, *your* power all along."

"But they are responsible for some things."

"The dark things, Sam. The drinking of blood. The fear of light. The ugly nails."

"Hey."

"Sorry."

I said, "Everyone makes fun of the nails until they need their Amazon packages opened."

He laughed lightly. "I suspect—and I could be wrong—that some of their own particular talents leak through, too. My mother, for instance, was particularly gifted at mind reading, which is where my own skills come from."

"And Tammy's," I added.

"Yes, Sam. I suspect my mother's talents in this area have spilled over to me, and now to your daughter... and to anyone you remain in close contact with."

I shook my head. It made perfect sense now why only he and my daughter, as humans, could read my mind; that is, the mind of an immortal. The bitch was powerful.

"Very powerful, Sam," he said, picking up my thoughts.

"Wait. Then why doesn't her gift of mind reading spill over to me, too? Or more fully spill over to me? I mean, I'm good at it, but nothing like my daughter. Or you."

He thought about that. "I don't think she can control the spillover, Sam, or how one utilizes it. I suspect if you worked hard enough at telepathy, you would get better and better at it."

"But not as good as you and my daughter."

"Probably not. Some of us do seem to have a

natural knack for it."

"Lucky you."

"Not necessarily. It's not easy hearing every single thought, from every single creature, alive and dead, within many square miles."

My jaw dropped. "You're kidding."

"I wish I was."

"And my daughter is the same?"

"From what I'm gathering, yes."

"How do you keep from going insane?"

"I turn it off as often as possible."

"But when it's on, you can hear... everything?"

"Every thought—and sometimes I can even feel the corresponding emotion, too, if the emotion is strong enough."

"Sweet mama."

"You can say that again."

But I didn't say it again. I was thinking of my poor daughter and wondering like crazy how she keeps it all together, too.

The Alchemist, of course, was aware of my thoughts. "There is a chance, Sam, that she is more powerful than even me."

"Which makes her situation even worse," I said.

"Yes and no. Yes, she might have a bigger range... but she also might have greater control of it, too."

"Greater control?"

"She might be able to direct it more, perhaps. Turn off parts of it, for example."

"Your mother... wow. She must have been a sight to behold."

He looked away. "You have no idea."

I didn't need to be a mind reader to know I'd hit a nerve. Or seeing what I thought I was seeing. "You fear her," I said.

"Let's say that I have a healthy respect for her," Maximus said. "But I do not fear her, no."

Except I might have seen otherwise in his eyes. Something had flashed across them. Something furtive. It was, I was certain, the first and only time I had seen the Librarian display anything other than *quiet strength*. Something deep inside me chuckled. It was a feminine chuckle devoid of warmth; it quickly devolved into an animalistic growl. That this thing was within me was nearly too terrible to comprehend.

"Comprehend it, Sam. Understand it. Bear it. You have to. You are, quite frankly, single-handedly keeping one of the most dangerous people to have ever walked this earth at bay."

"No pressure or anything," I said.

He smiled lightly, and the nervousness he had displayed was gone. "Nothing you can't handle, my friend. Remember, you are much more than her."

"My Hermes bloodline."

"That and more."

"My own soul," I said.

"Yes, Sam. Your pure and loving soul is no match for the darkness that is her."

I paused, cocked my head, for I heard the words clearly. "She says she will break me. She will find a way. And I will be gone. Forever."

Some of the color drained from his face. "She is wrong, Sam. You can't believe her."

"I don't," I said. "I just packed her down even deeper. Locked her up real good."

I looked at him; he looked at me. He gave me a small but sad smile. I gave him the same smile. Finally, he said, "You are here about the creator?"

"God?" I said.

"No, your client."

I blinked at that. "My client? Charlie Reed?"

"Yes, Sam. He's a creator, and we need to talk about him. Now."

17.

Allison and I were jogging.

"So you're telling me you're just like me then?" she asked, phrasing the question only slightly different than the six other times she'd asked it.

"Insecure? No," I said.

"Sam..."

"Look, I'm not a witch, and have no desire to be a witch. I'm not even sure what the hell a witch does."

"Now you're just being mean. You've seen what I can do."

"And you're just learning," I said. "And you've been at this, what, a couple of years now?"

"There's lots to learn. Lots of spells. Lots of memorizing—"

I waved my hand. "Nope. Not for me."

"According to Millicent, you used to be quite good at it."

"And she knows this how?"

Millicent was, of course, part of Allison's triad. Millicent was also a ghost. She was also, apparently, once a good friend of mine—we all were—down through the ages, in various incarnations, living as witches on the fringes of civilizations.

"Not always the fringes, Sam. But we were rarely, if ever, accepted. We did what we had to do, to stay alive. Historically, witches weren't exactly looked upon favorably. And to answer your question, Millicent has access to information we don't readily have at our fingertips."

"Because she's dead," I said.

"Right. She has read each of our Akashic records. She knows exactly what we have done, lifetime after lifetime."

"Sounds like she has a lot of time on her hands."

"You don't like Millicent," said Allison.

I shrugged, which might have been lost during the jogging. "She sounds like a know-it-all."

"She does know it all! She's in spirit. She has access to knowledge we can never fathom—"

"Doesn't seem too hard to fathom a trio of witches running around a bubbling cauldron in the forest."

Allison slapped my shoulder. "You're just mad because Millicent doesn't want me to speak with you."

I shrugged. "I agree. She's a bitch."

"I didn't agree she was a bitch!"

"You were thinking it."

"Sam Moon. You have no idea what I'm thinking these days."

"Right," I said. "Because of the know-it-all bitch."

"Well, you can be mad at her, but you damn well know that her motives are well-meaning. The thing inside you—"

"Elizabeth," I said, surprised at how quickly I was defending the 'thing' inside me, and realizing just how deep my annoyance with Millicent ran.

"Well, we can't have Elizabeth privy to what we are doing. We aren't exactly on the same side, you know."

I opened my mouth to argue, but there was no argument. Allison—and freakin' Millicent—were right. Elizabeth heard everything I heard, despite how deep I stomped her down into my psyche. And each day, while I slept, Elizabeth was free to roam and divulge any secrets I might have been privy to, including Allison's thoughts.

"You were great friends with her, Sam. She told me that you and she were even closer than you and I are now."

I was about to make a snide remark that maybe Allison and I weren't as close as she thought, but I caught the hurt look in her eye. Allison was my best friend, and I trusted her with my life. Simple as that.

"And I trust you, Sam. With mine."

I nodded, and we continued jogging, the full afternoon sun hitting us at an angle. I felt... uneasy, but nothing I couldn't handle. Without this magical ring, I would be feeling a great deal of pain. Now, I just ran with a bearable sense of discomfort.

I glanced at Allison. "Millicent and I were really as close as you say?"

"Yes, Sam. And it breaks her heart that we aren't together again and that..." she let her voice trail off.

"We will never be together again?"

"Yes, Sam."

"How's Ivy working out?"

"She's eager. Impetuous. Gifted. So far, a good fit. But, according to Millicent, we're not quite as powerful as we had been with you. The three of us, Sam... the three of us could take on whole armies in the past. Could take down kingdoms. You should hear Millicent's stories of our victories."

"And of our defeats?"

Allison nodded. "There were many of those, too. And most were not pleasant at all."

"Why doesn't Millicent come around?" I asked.

"I asked the same question, Sam. Although she is getting better and better at manifesting—and there are times you would swear she was a flesh-and-blood woman—she doesn't feel that she is strong enough to..."

"Resist Elizabeth?" I asked.

121

"Resist you, Sam. She says there will come a time when you will fully utilize all that Elizabeth can offer you—and powerful, wide-ranging telepathy will be part of it."

I opened my mouth at that, then closed it again. "How does she know that?"

"As a spirit... she has access to *possibilities*."

"Like Nostradamus?" I asked.

"Something like that, yes. She has seen a number of possibilities for you, Sam. And in one of them, you have fully accepted all that Elizabeth can offer you."

"You mean Elizabeth has taken me over?"

"In one such scenario, yes. In one, you have lost, and Elizabeth has won. But in another... in another, you are a sort of a team, and you are damn near impossible to stop."

"Jesus," I said, and as I uttered the name, I felt a shift in me. Elizabeth didn't like the name Jesus. She shied away from it, sinking deeper into the darkness. Good to know.

We jogged in silence, and I found myself thinking long and hard about a trio of witches, born together throughout the ages, fighting the good fight against the powers that be—and a darker enemy yet. Millicent had purposely come forth into this incarnation before, and lived a full, rich life, all while Allison and I bided our time... wherever spirits bided their time. Heaven? Yes, maybe. The plan this time around had been to have Millicent available to us in spirit—and thus available to far more knowledge than we would normally have access to. It was a noble plan... until I went and got turned into a vampire. Never fear, there was an understudy in the wings, a fourth girl who was often reincarnated with us, a sort of helper. That fourth girl was Ivy Tanner, and thus she was invited to take my place. I wasn't sure I liked her either, come to think about it.

"I think it's cute when you get jealous, Sam."

"Oh, shut up."

She grinned and jogged easily next to me. Her caramel skin glistened. My own mostly pale skin glistened too. I felt sunburns come and go, come and go, over and over and over again. But yet my skin mostly remained alabaster white. When I finally got out of the sun, any sunburn that lingered would disappear like water evaporating on hot pavement.

"Tell me about your client," said Allison. "The creator."

And so I did. According to the Librarian, there were only so many creators. Most creators didn't know they were creators. More often than not, they tended toward the arts; in particular, writing and filmmaking, although a handful of them had created particularly immersive video games. The *particularly immersive* part was the key, for the creators among us had a unique gift. A very, very unique gift.

"They create worlds?" asked Allison, grabbing my arm and pulling me to a stop. She had timed it perfectly, for there was a short, wind-blown, stunted tree next to us. We each opened our water bottles, took a swig, and leaned against the tree.

"It's complicated," I said. "But that's the whole of it."

"You mean *real worlds*?"

"I mean real worlds. It's complicated," I said again.

"Then uncomplicate it, Sam. Because this is big. And it's kind of freaking me out."

I explained it as best as I could. According to Maximus, there were only a half dozen or so creators in our world at any given time. Almost none of them were aware of their talents, which was not necessarily a bad thing.

"They are accidental creators?"

"In a way, yes. Although their works of art are no accidents."

"Sam, I need to be clear here. Are you telling me that Charlie Reed, the guy we met just the other night, can create... people?"

I took another swig of water and grinned at her. "Not just people, Allie. He can create whole worlds."

18.

Tammy liked to test herself.

Most often, she liked to test her *range*, especially since it always seemed to be expanding. These days, she was certain it was about a mile in either direction, although she wasn't entirely sure how far a mile was. People who drove cars always seemed to know how long a mile was, and since she was supposed to get her driver's license soon, maybe she would soon know just how far a mile was. Heck, maybe it was even two miles!

She shrugged at that. One, two, or even three, it didn't really matter. She only knew that it was far. Like real far.

Even now, with her tuners (as she thought of it) stretched out as far as they could go, she was fairly certain that she was picking up the thoughts of a homeless man crossing the street in front of the Hungry Bear on Harbor and Bastanchury. His thoughts were faint, almost too faint to hear, but she tuned into them anyway, because why not? She was bored, sitting here alone on her front porch, with the sun angling directly into her eyes, while her mother was off jogging with Allison, and probably drinking too much—and certainly talking too much.

The man crossing the street was hungry. Tammy couldn't yet feel others' *emotions*—she tried to do that once, when she had heard about 'empaths'—but she could certainly *hear* his thoughts, and he was wishing like crazy that someone would come out of the Hungry Bear and maybe give him their leftovers. God, he was so hungry. He wasn't sure when he'd last eaten. And then his thoughts briefly spun out of control and she saw static, and she was pretty certain the man was insane. In her mind's eye, she briefly saw what he saw: the restaurant and customers and cars and static. Now he sat on a step, near the restaurant, and hoped for help.

Tammy tuned out again. The homeless guy was bumming her out.

The Hungry Bear was, like, far away. A long, long walk for sure. Even a long bike ride!

Tammy was certain her range had just increased again, even from the last time she tested it just a few days ago. There was, of course, something else she'd been meaning to test, something that even she was kind of scared to test.

But, what the heck? No time like the present, as her mom always said.

That coming from someone who was immortal. From someone who had all the time in the world. And Tammy knew her mom was immortal, too. She knew it, and could see it. Her mom, like, never aged. Never even a little. Her mom still looked as young as ever, all the way back as far as Tammy could remember. Tammy knew her mom had been attacked when she was thirty-one years old. That had been over ten years ago. Tammy, now at sixteen-years-old, knew that she would someday look the same age as her mom. And then, after that, Tammy would start looking *older* than her mom.

So weird, she thought, as she looked now for her first victim.

She found it within seconds. It was a busy sparrow working its way through the neighbor's tree, twittering occasionally, hopping from branch to branch, pausing briefly and cocking its little head this way and that.

Tammy tuned into it.

Or tried to.

She got nothing. Static, if anything. The same kind of static she had just gotten from the homeless guy. She wasn't sure what the static meant. Maybe she wasn't receiving the signal correctly? She focused more, and found herself squinting. A small noise came from somewhere at the back of her throat. Jesus, was that a grunt? She didn't know, and didn't really care. In fact, there was only one thing she cared about, and that was the bird sitting on a nearby branch, presently grooming its wings.

You've really gone off the deep end this time, Tam Tam, she thought. The deep end of what, she didn't know. Just another stupid saying adults had.

Deep end or not, she didn't care. It was fun exploring her gifts. It was fun, quite frankly, being her. In fact, despite all the crazy, gross and illegal things she'd heard in hundreds if not thousands of people's minds, she would still want to be herself over anyone else on the planet. Including Allison!

Her mind was drifting. She knew it. She focused again, squinting more, and, yes, there was another small grunt at the back of her throat. She didn't know why she grunted, but it seemed to clear her mind.

Focus, Tammy. Focus.

She heard... something. No, she *felt* something. Something powerful. Something nearby. Something, somehow, above her, too. No, around her. But that didn't make sense. She focused some more, and felt it again. Yes, definitely above her, and maybe around her too. But she was sketchy on that last part, as it didn't make sense. More than anything, she sensed patience. An eternal patience. And something else.

Possession. Not like the kind of possession Mother or Kingsley or Fang dealt with, but ownership. Whatever was above and around her felt entitled to something. Whatever that something was. And just as she pondered the sensation, Tammy knew immediately what it was. Something nearby felt entitled to *her mother*. Felt as if it *owned* her mother. It felt very strongly about this. But it was so patient. So... damn... patient.

And then she lost it, whatever it was. She tried to capture it again, but it seemed just to elude her. Whatever it was, she suspected it was still nearby.

She knew her mother had made an arrangement with her one-time guardian angel, Ishmael, to watch over the two of them; in particular, Anthony, since, supposedly, Tammy still had her own guardian angel. Tammy wasn't sure what to think about guardian angels. She never heard them or saw them or felt their presence. She probably would never have believed in them, if her own mother didn't have, like, a weirdo relationship with one. Yes, Tammy had *seen* the angel in her mother's memory. And Ishmael was, well beautiful. Lordy, he was handsome. Heck, if she had an angel just like Ishmael, she would sure as heck choose him over the hairy Kingsley. Then again, Kingsley was sort of hunky in his own way. And, for all she knew, he was just as strong as any angel.

Still, her mother's guardian angel was radiant. And powerful. And devoted. And obsessed. Then again, she'd never personally seen him and had never tried to tune into him, if that even possible.

That is, until now.

It was him. She was sure of it.

How could something so beautiful and epic and old and powerful be so hung up on her mom?

Her regular old mom?

Tammy didn't know. She also knew that guys were weirdos. Like, big weirdos. Even supernatural guys. Probably even angels, too. She had seen the things guys lusted for, hungered for, and were willing to hurt and to kill for. Most of it centered around women. Or weird sex. Somehow, her mother had gotten under the angel's skin—if they had skin—and he'd been willing to give up his place in heaven for her. As in, his stature as her guardian angel. What he was now, Tammy didn't know. But hadn't she also just felt his darkness, too? His strange obsession? Yes, she had. It was there, brewing, and it didn't feel very different than the kind of darkness she felt from ordinary men she came across every day.

Tammy spent some time clearing her head. As she did so, she couldn't help but feel sorry for her mother, too. Boy, what a hornet's nest her mother had walked into—or jogged into—all those years ago. One night of jogging—and a vicious attack later—had opened up worlds not just to her mother...

But to all of them.

Some good had come from it. But also a lot of strange crap, too. Tammy, admittedly, liked some of the strange crap. No, she liked all of it. Well, maybe not the parts where people got hurt or killed. But she liked the mystery of it all. The excitement of it all. The potential of it all.

She reminded herself to focus again. And again.

Finally, she got her head back to the subject of the bird. A bird that had been replaced by another bird or two, during all that thinking. The bird, she knew, had to be there, in her thoughts. Logic suggested it would be. All she had to do was find a way in. Or, more accurately, to *understand* how to get in. And once she was in, she suspected, she could get in over and over and over again.

As far as she knew, no one, but no one, could do what she could do, although Tammy always suspected the Librarian might have similar gifts. Gifts that rivaled hers, or exceeded them.

Focus, Tammy!

More static. Now a break in the static. Now more static. Ugh, this wasn't going according to plan. The static looked like snow. The same kind of snow she would sometimes see on the TV when there was a bad connection. Maybe she was wrong, maybe she wasn't able to slip into the mind of a bird...

The static wavered, then disappeared—and was replaced with something peaceful, calm, excited, eager, hungry, curious, adventurous, hungry, hungry, hungry...

There. A small movement in the grass.

Movement, movement, movement.

Hunger, excitement, eagerness, patience.

Patience, patience.

Now! Now! Now!

Flight, soaring, attack, pounce, snip, scoop, swallow.

Triumph, eagerness, and now flight. Beautiful, easy, effortless flight.

Tammy opened her eyes, blinked hard. Her last image was of telephone wires, and then endless sky, and the Earth far below...

She grinned, then gagged. After all, she'd experienced the sensation of finding a roly-poly bug, snipping it in half, and then swallowing each half. And loving every minute of it.

"So very gross," she said, wiping her mouth.

Of course, it was also incredibly, wonderfully, insanely awesome.

She was just about to find another bird—she liked the way they thought, she liked how each movement was clean and calculated and pure and eager—when she caught wind of another thought.

A thought that was pure evil.

19.

We were on Main Street in Huntington Beach.

One of my detective friends lived in an apartment above this very street. My detective friend probably enjoyed living above mere mortals, like a feudal lord. My detective friend tended to think highly of himself. My detective friend also had a heart of gold. My detective friend would probably agree with all of the above.

"Say, doesn't Knighthorse live around here?" asked Allison, who, I was certain, was crushing on the man. She tended to crush on all the men in my life.

"Not true," she snapped.

"Not even a little?" I asked.

"Okay, maybe a little."

My kids were at home, taking care of themselves, which is why I had my ringer on high and my phone in my hand. Three months ago, Allison had been the one to tell me that someone had abducted Anthony from middle school. No mother—supernatural or not—could deal with another call—or text—like that. Ever. Again.

Which was why my ex-guardian angel, Ishmael, continued standing watch nearby. True, Tammy's own guardian angel was on the job, but he seemed to have a far more hands-off approach than I was comfortable with. Anthony's own guardian angel had long since abandoned his post—thanks to my son's brief foray into immortality all those years ago, back in the hospital, back when I had temporarily turned him into a vampire to save his life. Now, with Ishmael standing guard over them, I could rest easy.

Or try to. After all, not too long ago, Ishmael was ready to abandon Anthony, claiming my teenage son was now perfectly capable of taking care of himself. Um, 'scuse me? I'd reminded the fallen angel (or *exiled* angel, as he called himself) that the devil himself was sniffing around. Well, Ishmael had seen the logic of my argument and, thus far, had continued keeping watch.

Of course, what the fallen angel was actually capable of doing, I wasn't entirely sure. I suspected he possessed great strength. I also suspected he couldn't be killed, like ever, in any way, shape or form, silver or no silver. Stake or no stake. Ishmael, after all, was a spiritual being who could summon a physical body. And from what I understood, spiritual beings couldn't die.

But some of us get reabsorbed, I thought, as we found an outdoor seat at Chi Chi, along the busy, busy sidewalk.

"Reabsorbed sounds so... gross," said Allison.

"Well, that's how I see it," I said.

"But that's not how it was actually phrased," she said, having earlier relived my experience again with God. "Return home, I believe, were the words used."

"Return home, reabsorbed, winking out of existence. It all feels the same. It all feels like crap."

The patio was jam-packed. Luckily, a hum of conversation in the air mostly drowned out our words. Our very strange words.

"It's not crap, Sam. It may not be heaven, but it's also something else. I suspect it's total and complete bliss, with access to all that is and ever will be. I suspect it's peace and joy magnified thousands and thousands of times. Millions of times. Sam, you would be going home to God."

"Can we change the subject?" I asked.

"Sure," she said. "Besides, I don't think you're ever gonna die. You're just too... nasty."

"Nasty?"

"I mean that in a good way."

"There's a good nasty?"

"There's feisty nasty. Street-smart nasty.

There's a nasty that doesn't take shit from anyone, and always, always beats the bad guy in the end."

"Even if the bad guy is my ex-husband currently hiding out in my son?"

"Maybe that's just the thing, Sam. Maybe it's time to forgive Danny and not think of him as the bad guy."

"He tried to kill me."

"He set you up."

"Is there a difference?"

She thought about it. "Maybe not. Either way, we can agree he made poor choices in the past."

"The poorest of choices. And I thought he was long gone, and now he's back, and he's living in my son, and I have no way to remove him..."

To remove him meant journeying into my son's own mind, which I had no access to. Of course, there was also the small problem of my son wanting his father around. Liking his father around.

I knew the devil could arrange for my son's death, to get at Danny within, Danny, who had out-smarted the devil once, which was kind of funny if it wasn't so terrible, especially since Danny was-n't really all that smart, despite being an attorney.

Allison and I knew the devil had another angle too. Yes, the devil wanted Danny, but he wanted my son, too. In particular, access to my son's unusual gifts and strengths. What the devil wanted my son for, I hadn't a clue. But I think he saw my son as a sort of future thug, a henchman of sorts, capable of doing the devil's dirty business, which sounded about as terrible as it got.

"Maybe we should change the subject again," said Allison.

Meanwhile, our Moscow Mules were being served in sub-Arctic copper mugs that somehow made the ginger beer and vodka even more delicious. Too bad I couldn't get buzzed, or drunk, which, come to think of it, was probably a good thing. I'd read somewhere that drug addicts and alcoholics were susceptible to possession. Just as I thought that thought, a ripple of knowing rose up from the depths of my mind. Yes, Elizabeth was agreeing with me. And she should know. She and her misfit band of highly evolved dark masters had done a hell of a lot of possessing.

What was the point of all of that possessing anyway? What was the point of mastering the dark arts? Of controlling people? Of all the battles and wars? Of selling of your soul?

I directed all of the questions to Elizabeth herself, communicating directly with her for the first time in months. Of course, I knew she had done the *opposite* of selling her soul. She and those like her had bypassed the apparent natural order of things, to the unending irritation of the devil himself, who, apparently, could not lay a hand on them, much less find them.

Allison used this moment to excuse herself to the bathroom, mentioning something or other about this very much not being a conversation she wanted to be a part of. Then again, I wasn't really paying attention to her. When she left, I heard the words rise up from deep within me:

Power is overrated, Sssamantha. Control is what we are after.

Control of what?

Of all that is.

As I considered her words, a cold chill washed over me. God, I knew, was often referred to as all that is. Heck, Allison had just used the term.

You want to defeat God? I asked.

There is no God, Sam. There is only opportunity.

Excuse me, but I very likely just had a conversation with God.

Perhaps, Sam. But let me ask you this? Why does God seek to continuously expand? To continuously and forever more expand? What is it he seeks? Why does he use us so?

I, admittedly, had never delved into that question. I suspected it was because God was bored. Or whatever the equivalent of boredom was to something so powerful that it could create whole multiverses.

Never bored, Sam. God seeks to fill the Void.

Void?

That which isn't known.

Not following, sweet cheeks, I thought.

God is forming as we speak, expanding as we

speak, seeking as we speak.

Forming into what? Expanding into what? Seeking what?

We do not know, as of yet.

Although I didn't let the crazy bitch out much—or ever—I was still irrevocably connected to her. If I so chose, I could delve into her own mind. I never so chose. I was, quite frankly, frightened by what I might find. I really, really didn't want to know what was banging around in there, unless I had to, and so far I hadn't needed to. With that said, I caught her subtle impressions and sly nuances.

But you aim to find out? I said.

There is unlimited potential within that which you call God, Sssamantha. The source entity, as many call it, is so vast that even it does not know its boundaries.

And you seek to find his boundaries?

No, Sssamantha. I have no use for helping our source entity. No, I seek to lay claim to the unknown space, if you will.

And then what? I asked. *And here comes Allison, by the way. She really doesn't like you, you know.*

Elizabeth ignored me, perhaps reveling in her first taste of freedom in some time. No, not reveling. Making the most of it.

We can be gods, Sssamantha.

Why not lay claim to the moon, or some forgotten planet? Why not rule Mars and get the fuck off our planet once and for all?

We do not seek worlds, Sam. We seek to create them.

If you desire to expand into unknown realms of the universe, then why do you seek to return to the Earth?

Because we need a launching point. We need a home base. We need a gathering point. Where we are now we are without form and we are muted. We have been tamed.

I'd had enough. I shook my head and concentrated—turned out I had to concentrate harder than I'd expected, as Elizabeth was a devout believer of taking a mile when given an inch. She had filled my mind and thoughts.

Back you go, I thought. *Back, back.*

She went, but not willingly, and I threw up a half dozen more walls around her, sealing her deep in my mind.

"What was all that God business?" asked Allison, returning.

"I'm not sure you want or need to know," I said. "And no delving into my mind, either."

"Fine," she said. "Then can we get back to what we were talking about earlier? The part about Charlie being a creator? You sort of left me hanging there."

Our waitress came by and took our lunch orders.

"It's called a pregnant pause," I said when our waitress was gone.

"Why is it called that?" asked Allison. "Pregnant pause?"

"The calm before the storm?" I suggested.

"The storm being... a screaming baby?"

"Or a screaming mother."

"Well, then that was a full pregnancy, complete with a 20-hour labor pause. Now tell me: what do you mean he can create whole worlds?"

20.

It came again, and now Tammy was sitting up.

The thoughts—the very, very evil thoughts—were still a distance away. Maybe even as far away as the bum she could still hear at the Hungry Bear, the bum who was hoping not just for a little money but for some real food.

In fact, the roiling, dark, hate-filled thoughts were seeping past the bum even now. Stopping in front of the bum. The homeless man quit thinking of food or money or anything. Tammy sensed his fear. Worse, she almost *tasted* his fear. That was happening to her more and more these days. Sometimes she could taste an emotion, and if it was anything but happiness, it didn't taste good at all. Now she tasted sour, spoiled putrescence, as if she had bitten into a rotten hot dog filled with maggots. She nearly gagged. Where that maggot part came from, she didn't know.

Tammy had unknowingly brought her knees up and had wrapped her arms around them. She found herself rocking, rocking, rocking...

She felt the homeless man cowering, ducking his head, closing his eyes, and praying with all his heart—and as he prayed, she felt something slither up next to the man and whisper, "Soon..."

She felt the man lose control of his bladder, and now she was rocking even harder. Maybe moaning a little, too.

The evil swept onward, slithering, gliding, catching a breeze here and there. Sometimes it paused to watch people in their cars or cross the streets, and Tammy sensed one and all swallow suddenly and feel an irrational fear—and now the darkness continued onward, upward, gliding and blowing and drifting toward her.

Suddenly, she knew what was coming.

The devil.

***

"That's exactly what I mean," I said. "Whole worlds."

Allison's eyes searched my face, even as her mind searched my mind. I knew from experience that the more recent a conversation was, the sharper it was in one's memory. This should be sharp enough for her to mostly follow it.

"But I'm not following it, Sam," she said. "There's a lot of bouncing around going on in there. You sort of connected your conversation with Maximus to a lot of other things going on with your life right now. I'm untangling too many threads, threads that are leading to other threads, other conversations, other people. You're going to have to spell it out for me."

"My client Charlie Reed, an engineer at Raytheon and our new favorite writer, is part of a rare breed of humans on this planet."

"Creators?"

"Yes," I said.

"But don't all novelists create worlds?"

"They do," I said. "But not all are on the same level as Charlie Reed. Not all create the way he creates. Remember the word he chose, rather carefully, back in his office."

"Love," she said.

"He infuses his story with love. And I mean real love," I added. "Maximus thinks someone like Charlie might have spent years loving each and every character, years and years, before bringing them to the page."

"And so when he does finally write about them..."

"They are practically real, at least in his own mind."

"But that's just the thing, Sam. *In his own mind.*

You just said it."

"According to Max, creation is a funny business. Manifestation is a funny business. We all have the ability to create and to manifest. Some of us just do it better than others. Some of us are more clear-minded and impassioned. And some of us inadvertently channel real life-force."

"Wait, Sam. Are you stating he's creating *real life*?"

"I am. And he is."

"But..."

"Think of it as the perfect confluence of talent, love and manifestation."

"But he's just a man. He's not a god."

But even as she stated that, she caught something else in my thoughts—and perhaps even something she was already aware of. I smiled, waited.

"But we are all God," she said.

"And if we are all fragments of God, even tiny, tiny fragments, wouldn't it stand to reason that some of us, perhaps in varying degrees and strengths, can access the God source within us? That some of us could, perhaps, perform miracles beyond comprehension?"

"But he doesn't even know he's performing them, Sam. He thinks his house is haunted, for crissakes!"

"*Accidental* creation might just be the most powerful creation of them all."

"Where did you get that idea?"

"Just came to me," I said, sipping on my Moscow Mule. "I know from experience that trying too hard can screw something up."

"And maybe in Charlie's oblivion..."

"Creation is pouring through him unhindered."

"Unhindered?" she asked.

"It's a word," I said, "that I like to use from time to time."

"But why are you calling him a creator?"

"Whatever this original source entity is, wherever he came from and whatever he's trying to do, is invariably explored through more creation. More and more creation. We are such creations. And our creations are such creations. And onward and downward."

"So, in effect, someone like Charlie is helping God, by creating more?"

"Yes. As do all of us. We're all creating and manifesting, both big and small."

"I'm hardly manifesting, Sam. And I can't think of a single thing I've created."

"Everything is creation, Allie. The cook is creating our meals. Someone created this table and chairs. City planners created Main Street. You have sculpted and created your body. You have created the look you are wearing now. Someone, somewhere designed and created the clothing you are wearing. All of life is creation, an ongoing, never-ending flow of creation."

She blinked at me. Then blinked again. And kept on blinking until she finally said, "We're both crazy, you know that, right?"

"Life just might be crazier."

"So we're all creators in our own little way. Fine. Then explain how any of this actually helps God."

"I don't know, Allie. But whoever or whatever he, she or it has an unerring need to expand ever outward, out into infinity."

"Why?"

"If I had to guess—"

"And you do," said Allison, winking.

"I would think it is searching for itself."

"I'm not sure I'm following."

"I'm not sure I am either, Allie, but—and I believe this might be true—I was just recently told that even God doesn't know how big he is."

"And he wants to know?" asked Allie.

"Wouldn't you?"

"If I was God, who the hell knows. Wait, so you're saying that me putting my hair into a ponytail helps him to somehow expand into this unknowable place? You know, since I *created* my hairstyle and all." She winked again.

I looked at her and thought about it. "Yes," I said. "In a small way, it does. In a small way, watching his own creations creating something of their own, helps him expand out, incrementally, into forever."

"I think we need to start drinking more, Sam."

"Maybe," I said.

"And our friend Charlie?"

"He's doing even more creating. Perhaps on par with hundreds of thousands of us, all rolled into one."

"But if he's doing all that creating..."

"Where are his creations?" I asked, finishing her thought.

"Right. We know—or think—one of them is showing up at his house."

"And Max had a theory about that, too," I said. "The world of Dur, he suspects, is now very much a *real* world. Not here, exactly, but perhaps nearby. Perhaps side by side with our own."

"Like a parallel world?"

"Yes," I said.

"So why is Queen Autumn showing up *here*, in our world? Why doesn't she just stay in her own?"

"I don't know," I said. "But I think we need to ask her."

Allie looked at me. We both cracked a smile at about the same time. "The world of Dur is real, then?" she asked.

"I think so, Allie."

"King Philos? The Foul Wizard Xander? The First Knight Rory? All the warriors and ladies and squires... they're all real?"

"More than likely."

"Wait, Sam! Do you remember where Charlie

left off in the story?"

It didn't take me long to think about it. I, like Allison, was eagerly awaiting news about...

"Autumn's baby," I said, "was kidnapped."

"And now Autumn's here, supposedly haunting Charlie's hallway."

"But maybe she's not haunting," I said. "Maybe she's here for something else."

"Maybe she's looking for help."

I thought about that. Thought about it hard. Meanwhile, I didn't have to read Allison's own mind to know where it had drifted off to. She wanted to very much believe the world of Dur was real, and I didn't blame her. If it was real, then it was populated with characters that we had both come to love, even if their stories weren't finished. Yes, Charlie had done one hell of a job of creating a rich and magical world.

A helluva job.

"Sam, do we tell him?"

"Tell Charlie that he's a creator, that he holds hundreds, if not thousands, of people's lives in his hands?"

"Seems pretty heavy, I know."

I thought about her question, and kept thinking about it all through lunch.

21.

"What?" said Anthony, looking up. He'd been sitting on the floor with his knees up and his head covered by folded arms.

Tammy knew he'd been talking to his father for most of the day, as he had been doing for the past few months. Funny how she rarely came up in their conversations. She'd never been that close to her dad. He worked too much, was out too late, and when he was home, all he wanted to do was get on his computer and work even more... or play catch with Anthony. Or go on long walks with Anthony. Rarely did they ask her to join them. Other than a goodnight kiss on her forehead, Tammy didn't have too many memories of her father.

She told herself that she didn't care that her father almost never asked about her—at least in the conversations she listened to. These days, she mostly tuned out the two of them. She could only stand so much of Anthony's sports stories. Or how much he missed his dad. Or how he wished his dad was out of his head and standing here, with him. Her father, for his part, made no promises and only consoled Anthony, which she thought wasn't too terrible of him. It would be worse if he was making promises he couldn't keep.

Danny Moon was getting better at communicating with Anthony. Her father, she saw, was more lively and active these days, and seemingly resided in the very front of Anthony's psyche, unlike Elizabeth who resided very deep inside her mom.

Was her own father trying to take over Anthony's body? The way her mother feared Elizabeth was trying to do with her? Tammy didn't know. Her gut said no. Her gut said her father was simply excited to be active in their lives again. And equally relieved to not be in hell. And Anthony was just as excited to have his father with him again. Side by side. Two peas in Anthony's pod.

Now, as she stood in his doorway, she said, "Something's... coming."

"Yeah, my vomit if I have to keep looking at your face—okay, I know. Dad wants me to say sorry. Your face doesn't make me want to vomit... very much."

Tammy rolled her eyes. "Tell Dad to be quiet for a minute. And you shush too. Something—or someone—is coming. And I think it—he's—coming for you."

Anthony's green eyes narrowed, then widened, then narrowed again. "You look scared," he said.

"I am."

Truth was, Tammy was feeling a little... excited too. She wasn't a hundred percent sure she knew what the word *titillated* meant, but if it meant what she thought it meant, then that's what she was feeling. Tammy, of course, had never met the devil before. Only in her mother's and Anthony's memories. And the man who claimed to be the devil had been hunky as heck. Of course, she had also watched that same man explode into a bloody mist when the devil had made him walk in front of an oncoming train.

But he's the devil, Tammy reasoned. Maybe he could bring the hunky guy back? From the dead and all that.

"Tammy—do you hear it?"

She did. Whispering. Lots of whispering. Hundreds if not thousands of voices whispering. Foul whisperings, too. Dark whisperings, hate-filled whisperings. Tammy was suddenly certain that she was hearing a legion of demons.

She couldn't move. Vaguely she recalled her phone in her pocket. She knew she should call her mother. But she couldn't move. Couldn't think. The whispering... so evil, so vile, so determined to destroy.

"C'mon, Tam!" said Anthony, rolling up to his feet effortlessly. As he dashed forward, he grabbed her hand and pulled her along. His strength was undeniable. Tammy couldn't have resisted if she wanted to. As it were, she followed behind, sometimes stumbling. Aware that her brother moved like a jungle cat. Aware, also, that evil seemed to be pouring out of hell itself and showing up here, in their cul-de-sac.

She was back outside in the setting sun. Correction, the sun had just set. Her mother, she knew, would be at full power now. She blinked into the still-bright sky. The single tree in their yard swayed. Wispy clouds streaked the sky, like a paintbrush stroke. The street was empty, even of parked cars. Correction, not empty. There, down the street, maybe seven or eight houses away, was a lone jogger. A lone, female jogger, whose ponytail sashayed from side-to-side as she ran, whose hips moved in perfect rhythm to her churning arms. A jogger who kept her elbows in and hands up. To Tammy, the woman looked like she might have had some kick-boxing training or something. Then again, her mother had never bothered to take her to boxing or kickboxing lessons at Jacky's gym. After all, the universe didn't revolve around her, but it sure as heck revolved around her little brother.

"I don't see anything," said Anthony. "But I hear something, I think."

As the woman approached, her long shadow

stretched out before her. To Tammy, her shadow seemed maybe a little too long. And too narrow. And oddly shaped, too. Were those claws where her hands should be?

"It's her," said Tammy.

"Who?"

"The jogger!" she heard herself scream.

After all, the woman's very strange shadows had literally risen up from the sidewalk and became anything but shadows. They morphed into something three-dimensional and huge and far, far scarier in real life than she could ever imagine. Yes, Tammy had seen the three-headed hellhound in her brother's own memory—and even vaguely in her mother's memory, although her mother's memory had been a memory of a memory, and those were never very clear.

This was clear as day. This was real and it was happening now.

***

She heard her brother say, "Oh, my God," as what had once been a shadow grew in size, and its massive claws dug deeply into the sidewalk, tearing up concrete chunks and flinging them everywhere. The creature rocketed toward them and all Tammy could do was scream.

Or try to.

In fact, before anything could escape her lips,

something massive loomed over her. Something massive and fiery and towering over the house itself. Tammy knew what it was, but she was too frightened to look. Too frightened to think. Too frightened to do anything but close her eyes and finish that scream she had seemingly started so long ago.

The ground shook. A thunderous, cavernous roar froze her heart in place.

And as the ground shook harder and the cacophony of growls rattled her teeth—three growls, in particular—something superheated and bright flashed overhead. It could have been a lightning strike. It could have been a guardian angel racing to their rescue. But Tammy knew what it was. She had seen it before. It was the flash of a fiery sword.

And as it charged overhead, it was followed by an ungodly shriek that turned immediately into wails of agony. So loud, Tammy was certain that her eardrums would split open.

***

When Tammy cracked open her eyes, she saw the three-headed dog was now a two-headed dog and it was running in circles in her cul-de-sac.

The severed head lay not too far from their driveway, it massive bloody jaws snapping over and over. Jaws that finally stopped snapping. And not too far behind the injured mythological monster was the female jogger. To Tammy's eyes, the jogger had never missed a beat, and had continued her easy pace unerringly toward them.

There was a monster in front of her, a gravely wounded monster running circles in the cul-de-sac where she had played soccer as a kid, and baseball, and learned to rollerblade. Where Daddy and Anthony had played catch. Now, a devil dog ran seemingly blindly, shrieking loud enough to wake the dead.

But something was above her, too. Above and a little behind her, and it was glowing with a furious intensity. She saw the white light of it reflecting off the tree branches and leaves before her, the same tree the little bird had just been sitting in.

And somehow, through all the wailing, she heard a fire crackling directly overhead. Crackling and spitting and roaring as if she were sitting in front of the world's biggest fireplace. The now two-headed dog collapsed onto its front legs. Blood pumped from the open wound in the third neck, splashed over the ground. The nearest dog head tried desperately to lick the opening, but it seemed a futile effort, with all the blood.

Now, she slowly, slowly looked up.

And up.

Way up.

And saw fire, lots of fire. But the fire had shape too, the shape of a humanoid: two legs, arms, a torso, shoulders, a head. The head was a good deal taller than the roof of the single-story house. In its right hand, it held a fiery sword. In fact, where the hand ended and where the sword began was hard to discern.

She felt the heat, but it wasn't unbearable. She also felt the wind too, which seemed to emanate from the fiery entity standing over. The heat and wind swirled and blasted her. It also had a chemical smell that she was not familiar with.

From her vantage point, she could see white flames snapping and curling out from the entity's thighs and torso and chest and even his head. The flames turned to puffs of black smoke, and Tammy watched as blood sizzled on the burning sword. Sizzled and evaporated. There was a quiet calm about the entity standing over her. Perhaps strangest of all, she sensed her brother in there, looking out through an eyeless face, perceiving everything around them, including the demons that she could not see. Mostly, she sensed fearlessness and calm. Mostly, she sensed complete control and complete power.

Her brother's focus shifted from the demons and the wounded hellhound, to something lower to the ground. The flaming sword in his hand shifted into the on-guard position. Now Tammy heard clapping from the sidewalk. It was the female jogger, who now stood just beyond the chain-link fence that encircled their property, the same fence that the hellhound had effortlessly leaped.

"Okay, now that was badass," said the woman, as she continued to clap. "Seriously, I might not have seen anything like that in all my life. Except maybe when I watched you do the same to the werewolves. But this is no werewolf, is it? I have watched Cerberus single-handedly tear armies apart. In fact, until now, I had thought he was impervious to destruction. I guess I was wrong. Boy, was I wrong!"

Meanwhile, more dark blood pumped from the gaping opening, spreading like an oil slick across from the street. The creature's screeching had turned to high-pitched whimpering howls. How neighbors weren't pouring from their homes, Tammy didn't know.

She cocked her head, listening, searching. Okay, she did know. The homes were empty. In fact, *all* of the homes in the cul-de-sac were empty, even many of those that stretched further down the street too. What were the chances that all the homes on the street would be empty?

"Not very good," said the jogger, seemingly reading her mind. "Timing, after all, is everything."

The female jogger stood with hands on hips and caught her breath and took in the scene around her: the dying dog, the fire warrior towering behind her. Interestingly, Tammy could no longer detect her father's thoughts.

"Of course not, lass," said the jogger, her voice suddenly a little grittier than it had been a few moments ago. "Your father—the sniveling, coward-ly, no good rat bastard that he is—has been ejected to the Void."

Tammy didn't know what to think about the Void. The jogger before her was hard to read, but not impossibly so. The thoughts came quickly and were laced with fear and hate and anger and confusion. Mostly, there was something else going on. The jogger was thinking of... formulas? Arcane formulas. Secret formulas. All of which crowded her brain, filling the forefront of it enough so that Tammy couldn't push through.

"I can't have a little girl knowing my deepest, darkest secrets now, can I?"

The woman looked impassively upon the massive dog, which had dropped to its belly, whim-pering. The severed head had long since stopped snapping. "A shame. There are, after all, only so many three-headed dogs in the world."

"Will he die?" Tammy heard herself ask, although her voice might as well have been somewhere above her, somewhere in the area where the burning fire warrior was standing. But it was her voice, and it was distant and hollow and not quite filled with as much fear as she would have thought.

"Hard to say, lass. I've never seen anything hurt the old boy. I suspect he might power through. He is, after all, immortal too."

"Maybe he can get by with just two heads?"

"We'll have to see, lass. We are in uncharted

territory, so to speak."

"Why do you keep calling me lass?"

"It's a good word for a young girl with spunk."

"Spunk?"

"Grit."

Tammy nodded and thought she might understand. It was a compliment, maybe. The jogger smiled, and crossed her arms, and something on her arm *moved*. Tammy was sure of it. Something dark—a tattoo perhaps—undulated around the arm. She had seen it in her mother's memory, back when her mother had spoken to... the devil.

"You are a clever girl, aren't you?" asked the woman, pacing now just outside her gate. Tammy could see sweat stains around her armpits and nape of her neck. A steady and dizzying stream of strange formulas reached Tammy's inner ear. Tammy did her best to ignore them and push through them, but the strange words and ingredients only seemed to increase in intensity.

"Nuh uh, young lady. It's very rude to read someone else's mind without permission."

"You're doing it."

"That's because I invented being rude."

Tammy wasn't sure she was following.

"Never mind. It was a joke, lass. But let's just be clear: I can never, ever allow you into my mind. Ever. I am certain you would not like what you find there. I am certain it would drive you instantly crazy. Do you understand?"

Tammy wasn't so sure about that. Tammy, in fact, was quite intrigued with what she would find there.

There. Tammy briefly caught a train of thought, and, yeah, it wasn't a pretty one. The entity before her—the entity that might very well be the devil—had come to entice her brother. No, to *turn* her brother on everyone. Except, yes. The entity before her had just realized he/she might have come across a *new* target. A potentially better target.

The boy will not give up his father. The boy, at least in this form, scares the shit out of even me. The boy might be untouchable, at least for now. But the girl, ah, the possibilities...

And then the thought disappeared again, to be replaced by a long series of rambling codes and numbers and strange ingredients, effectively blocking out even Tammy's powerful telepathy.

"You heard that, didn't you?" asked the woman, who had resumed her pacing before the chain-link fence.

"You planted those words for me to hear," said Tammy.

Further down the road, a car turned down the street, headed in the opposite direction. Which was just as well. Tammy knew that if the driver looked in his rearview mirror, he would see a dying three-headed dog in her driveway. Oh, and a twenty-foot-tall fire warrior. Tammy also knew, after quickly dipping into the driver's head, that the driver had no intention of checking his mirror and was perfectly content to get off the road and into a shower.

"So, so, so powerful," said the woman.

"I'm just me," said Tammy, shrugging.

"Well, you, young lady, are the most powerful telepath I might have ever come across."

"That's not true," said Tammy, catching a quick snapshot into the woman's head. Or, rather, into the devil's head. "There was another, long ago."

"Yes. Very good."

"She had a son who was nearly as strong."

"Very, very good, lass."

"It is the same woman who possesses my mother."

"Indeed."

"You want her too."

"I want them all, little girl."

Tammy cocked her head and searched between the streaming, foreign words, words that she was certain were not in use in today's languages. They were, she was certain, a secret language that only a few knew, and fewer still knew how to use.

"So perceptive," said the woman.

"You are flattering me on purpose," said Tammy, for she had caught that as well, although the flattery came naturally to the entity before her. Using people came naturally. And so did hurting them. The entity before her enjoyed hurting them best of all. And if it couldn't hurt them, it enjoyed ruining them. And if it couldn't ruin them, it enjoyed scaring them. At the very least, it enjoyed being in their thoughts. Human thoughts, that was. No, that wasn't quite right. The entity before her *needed* to be in mankind's thoughts. Without which the devil would cease to exist.

"And we can't have that, right?" asked the jogger.

A picture appeared within Tammy's mind. It involved religion and the afterlife; heaven and hell; sinning and forgiveness; love and hate and fear. In particular, fear of the unknown. But mostly, the picture in her mind centered around *belief*. Belief in hell. Belief in the devil. Belief in punishment. Tammy understood that the entity currently pacing in front of her chain-link fence like a caged animal, had created an empire of fear. The empire was vast and multifaceted and reached down into the lives of most people, and for that, the entity was most proud and most grateful. Proud because of the work it had done, and grateful because it virtually guaranteed its continued existence.

Tammy wasn't sure if she was reading the devil's mind, or if the imagery was being purposely planted there. She suspected a little bit of both, as the codes and formulas were still there, but they seemed more in the background.

"So powerful," the woman said.

The tattoo had moved further down the woman's arm, just as it had when the handsome biker had been talking to her mother. Back then, her mother had watched the tattoo slowly undulate over the man's forearm. A living tattoo. It was, she was certain, the mark of the devil.

"You want to use me," said Tammy. "Or use my brother. Or use both of us. My mother, too, if you can."

The jogger stopped pacing, faced Tammy, and placed both hands on top of the chain-link fence. The tattoo had coiled tightly around her wrist. Somewhere inside the woman, through the chanting and stream of ancient words, she sensed a woman inside who had very much regretted making a deal with the devil, a woman who regretted losing all control of her body, a woman who was certain she might not live out the day, a woman who knew her own personal hell was being set up for her even now, with special tortures designed explicitly just for her.

"She chose poorly," said the devil, and Tammy heard the low growl now. It sounded nothing like how the jogger had sounded earlier. "She was nothing, just like the man before her. Lost souls, each. Adrift in this world, looking for a little excitement. I gave it to them, for a short while. But you are different, lass. We can work together. Your brother... your brother is a lost cause, I fear."

And in that moment, even through the strange verbiage, she saw what the devil saw. It was a brief glimpse of the future and it involved her brother helping those who couldn't help themselves. Her brother who would become a sort of urban legend. Whether the vision was true, she didn't know, but the devil seemed to believe it.

"Yes, lass. We can work together, me and you. I feel the darkness in you."

She opened her mouth to speak, but then closed it again. She was certain, no, she was *positive* that the devil was wrong. And yet, she felt a stirring in her. Something she couldn't quite put her finger on.

The woman standing at the fence smiled broadly, then raised her right hand. She snapped her fingers and something miraculous happened. The now two-headed hellhound was once again a three-headed hellhound. The severed head slowly disappeared from its resting place on the driveway, where its thick tongue had hung out. First it was there, and then, after a few seconds, it wasn't. The blood on the street disappeared too, and now the hellhound leaped to its feet, turned in a tight circle. The two original heads promptly snapped and bit and growled at the new head; soon, all three were fighting ferociously. Blood and fur flew.

"Kids," said the jogger, shaking her beautiful head. She looked from the devil dog and back to Tammy. "You think about what I said, lass, and I will be seeing you again."

She turned and jogged off, her ponytail swishing from side to side, her jogging form nearly perfect.

The three heads quit snapping at each other long enough to turn and growl at Tammy. Next to her, the fire warrior shifted, and now the dog turned and ran swiftly down the center of the street, only to disappear in the blink of an eye.

22.

I came home and the kids were being very well behaved.

As in, both were in their rooms, and both were doing their homework. No fighting, nothing broken, no blood, no TV blaring, no video games, no YouTubing, and their phones lay quietly next to them, seemingly forgotten. Both smiled at me when I checked in on them, although Tammy rolled her eyes. Gee, I wonder where she got that from?

She was about to turn the page of her textbook when she paused, looked up at me. "You know what happened."

"Of course I know."

"Who told? Wait. Your angel," she said, obviously scanning my mind.

"Not exactly my angel, not anymore, but that's

another story." Ishmael had appeared in my mini-van, in the passenger seat next to me. Although he had waited for me to stop at a stoplight, his sudden appearance had elicited a scream that I wasn't very proud to admit had come from my mouth.

"It was nothing, Mom, really. We had it under control."

"You had the devil under control?" I heard the words as I spoke them and could only shake my head.

"Then you probably have some idea what happened to the dog. Anthony took care of it. I wasn't scared."

My son, the fire warrior. I took in some air and continued processing the information I had been given by Ishmael only a few miles ago. Ishmael had, of course, been by their side, invisible, ready to fight, although my son, apparently, hadn't needed much help. If anything, I sensed awe from Ishmael, although it was hard to sense anything from a being that might not have real emotions. Certainly not human emotions.

"I can't believe your angel told on us. What a snitch!"

"Snitch? You're irritated that my ex-guardian angel told me that the devil had visited you. That the devil, in fact, had had a nice little conversation with you; that the devil, in fact, had enticed you?"

"Quit being so dramatic, Mom. It was nothing."

Except my guardian angel had said otherwise.

My guardian angel had sensed Tammy's interest, even as she tried to resist it. I didn't have to voice this, knowing Tammy had picked up on my thoughts and memory of my conversation with Ishmael.

"Geez, Mom, if you think about it... who wouldn't want me on their side? I can read anyone's thoughts, even your angel's, even animals. Besides, your angel can't read *my* mind. Only your mind. He doesn't know what I was really thinking."

"And what were you really thinking?"

"That the devil was a big weirdo."

I sensed evasiveness. Pure, motherly instinct. "Were you or were you not interested in what the devil had to say, young lady?" And the fact that I was having this conversation, really, *really* pissed me off to no end. I needed to speak with the devil, and I needed to do so now.

"No, Mom. He's long gone now."

"He's not as far away as you think."

"The lady that he's using—"

"Possessing."

"Okay, whatever. She's busy doing other things for him right now."

"And you know this how?"

She opened her mouth to speak. But then closed it again.

"Tell me now, young lady, or so help me, you will never see the light of day again."

"Like you?"

I glanced at the alchemy ring on my hand that let me go into the sunshine and not get fried. "Never mind that. Answer me."

She bit her lower lip, and I didn't have to read her mind to know what was going on: she was deciding how much to tell me.

"It's not that, Mom."

"So what's going on then, young lady?"

"Ever since I connected with the devil—"

"You connected, why?"

"I didn't mean to. I felt him coming. Felt a sort of pulse of evil coming. I don't know. I tuned into it, to see what it was."

"Okay." I waited.

"And ever since I tuned into it, it hasn't really gone away."

"What hasn't gone away?"

"My connection," she said.

"To the devil?"

"Yes. In particular, to the woman he's using."

"And she's where?"

"In Santa Ana."

"Doing what?"

"Working as a prostitute."

"And you can see this?"

"Yes."

"I command you to stop seeing this."

"Whatever, Mom."

"I mean it."

"Fine, I will."

"Block him. Something."

She opened her mouth to speak, paused, then looked away, and I suspected she couldn't block him. Not at the moment. At least, not for as long as the woman lived.

My daughter caught my eye again, and her simple look confirmed my suspicion. The devil and she were connected, at least, for the time being.

"Baby," I said, "you have to resist him."

"I will, Mommy. I swear."

"Does he talk to you?"

"No, not really."

"What does that mean?"

"I can feel him sort of, well, sort of checking in on me."

I looked at my cute little daughter with the haunted look in her eye, knowing that few would know just how haunted it was. For the first time in a long time, I didn't know what to do to help my baby.

"It's okay, Mommy. Everything will turn out okay," she said, and held my gaze. Then she turned back to her book.

I didn't like the way she held my gaze, and I especially didn't like what I thought I saw just behind her pupil. The smallest hint of fire.

23.

All this was because Danny—that worthless piece of shit—had turned tail and hid in his own son.

Yes, I knew my daughter was reading my mind, even through her door—hell, even if I was a mile or two away. Which is exactly why the devil wanted her. How much mind reading he could do, I didn't know. He didn't appear to have access to my mind back when I'd first met him at the Jamba Juice. If not, then, of course, he needed Tammy. And like my daughter said, *anyone* would want to use her. Hell, how valuable would she be in the hands of the government? Spy agencies? Criminal organizations? Other immortals? All would want her, all would exploit her, all would use her up and, ultimately, destroy her. The devil, I suspected, was just one of many who might come knocking. He'd just happened to be the first. And, perhaps, the most persuasive. And, perhaps, the nastiest.

If I can deal with the devil, I thought, *I can deal with anything. And if you are listening, Tammy, and I know you are, then hear this: I will fight for you until my last dying breath, whether you hate me or not, I will not lose you.*

I stood there in the hallway, just outside her door, trying to decide what to do next. Ultimately, I glanced at another door. My son's door.

***

"Knock, knock," I said, slowly easing the door open. One thing I knew about teen boys: they could be doing homework one moment, and something else entirely the next. That something else is why moms everywhere knock, pause, then open the door slowly. Real slowly. Of course, I took even further precautions...

"You can open your eyes, Mom. Sheesh, I'm just doing homework."

I prayed like hell Danny was giving our son privacy, too, if that were even possible.

"Hi," I said, stepping in and shutting the door behind me, although a shut door was a moot point with Tammy's eavesdropping.

And you should really mind your own business, I thought.

"You okay, Mom?"

173

"Yes, I'm okay. I was just telling Tammy that she really needed to mind her own business."

"Does she ever talk back? You know, like in your mind? The way I can hear Daddy?"

I frowned at his enthusiasm. "No, I don't think she can do that. She just listens."

"Yeah, I didn't think so. I've never, you know, *heard* her. But I can kind of feel her in there sometimes. When I catch her snooping around I just think of Miss Penelope."

I knew the name. "Your English teacher?"

"My *pretty* English teacher. Trust me, all I have to do is think of Miss Penelope and Tammy shoots right out of there, ha ha. Then I can usually hear her gagging in her bedroom. That's what she gets for spying on me."

I giggled, despite what I was hearing. Pretty clever way to get rid of his snooping sister. No teenage girl really wanted to know what's going on in the mind of their teenage brother.

"Well, don't you think Miss Penelope is a little old for you?" I asked.

"It's just a fantasy, Mom. Sheesh, that's what Dad said, too, but then he told me all about a crush he'd had on his math teacher. You should hear the nickname they had for her."

"I'd rather not," I said. I blinked and gathered myself, slightly taken aback by my son's candidness.

Unlike me and other immortals, my son hadn't

been possessed by a highly evolved dark master. Now, thanks to Danny, my son presently sported his own dark master in training, as I understood it. Although the thought of Danny being a dark master at anything nearly made me pee myself.

Highly Evolved Douchebag, I thought, and immediately heard the burst of laughter from down the hallway. From Tammy's room.

"Hey, what's so funny?" asked Anthony. "Why's Tammy laughing?"

"It's nothing," I said.

"Are you two making fun of me?"

"No, sweetie. Never."

He looked at me from over crossed arms, his muscular chest pushed up nearly to his chin. His forearms rippled, pulsed. I think he might have grown an inch since the last time I saw him, but that was probably my imagination. Each and every day, he looked more and more like the man he would become, and less like the boy he had just been.

"I want to talk about you, Anthony. Is that okay?"

He shrugged. "If you want."

I sat down on the floor in front of him. I said, "You saw the dog again today."

He nodded. My son was many things, but one of them wasn't telepathic, although his actual *hearing* seemed to be stronger than most.

"Are you okay?" I asked. "You weren't hurt?"

Anthony shook his head.

"This was the second time you turned into the fire man, right?"

"Fire warrior, Mom. And yes."

"Do you... do you have any questions?"

"Where does he come from? Is he always waiting for me?"

I thought about how to answer that, fully aware that Danny was also looking through my son's own eyes, fully aware that I was talking to two people at once, and not liking any of it. Then again, that's how Allison felt, too, wasn't it? Allison felt that she was talking to two people: myself and Elizabeth. No matter how deep I stamped down the demon bitch within my mind, she was always there, listening. Which was why Allison had cut me off from her thoughts. And I didn't blame her one bit, although it annoyed me to no end.

It was the same with Kingsley, Fang, Dracula, Franklin... we all had entities within us. We all had entities listening and conspiring later, while we slept. One thing I had learned in the past few years was that all immortals, or partial immortals like Kingsley, slept like the dead, whether during the day or night. Either way, we were dead to the world—and during that time the entities within us were free to leave, and free to return from whence they came. And from whence they came was a place beyond time and space, apparently, a space safe from the devil himself. Where this place was, I didn't know. But I suspected it was created from the ether and given life, somehow, similar to how Charlie Reed had created his own fantasy world.

With enough vision. With enough determination. And enough love—and perhaps even hate—a world could spring forth from those adept at such things.

I thought of all of this and more as my son looked on, and just behind his eye, I could see a small flame dancing. A very, very small flame. Nearly nonexistent. Surely, I would have missed it before, had I not known to look for it. The flame, I knew, was an indicator of my son's possession. Of Danny, his own father, watching us.

"You can ask him," I finally said.

"Ask the fire warrior?" Anthony's eyes widened.

"Yes. When you are ready, try talking to him. He will tell you who he is, and where he's from, because I don't know."

"Is he an alien?"

"In a way, yes. But you will need to ask him."

"You think he speaks American?"

I gave my son a half smile, waited.

"English! I meant English."

"He will understand you," I said. "And you will understand him. Language won't be a problem."

"Okay, I will do that someday. Maybe. The problem is, he's so dang big. I mean, I could see on top of the roof, Mom. You should have seen me."

"And no neighbors saw you?"

Anthony shook his head vigorously. "No one. The street was empty. It was like the devil knew."

"The jogger?"

"Yes. It was the same person I met in the warehouse. Just different bodies. She had the same weird tattoo. And the same dog!"

"And you weren't afraid?"

"With the fire warrior, I don't think I will ever be afraid again. And even without him, I think I can take care of myself. In fact..."

He paused, turned red.

"What, baby?" I asked.

"I think I can take him."

"The devil?"

Anthony nodded, vigorously at first, but then looked away, perhaps hearing his own words again. I let it go. That my son was confident was a good thing. I had seen the video where he had taken on four or five men at once—and not just any men— unchanged werewolves. Like me, Kingsley was supernaturally strong in his day-to-day life, too. And so had those men, many of whom had been flattened by my thirteen-year-old son.

"Anthony, do you know why the devil came today?"

"He's looking for Daddy."

I nodded. Anthony knew that, of course. Hell, the devil himself had spelled it out to Anthony back in the warehouse months ago, back when the devil had given my son a fighting chance to live. The devil had—and this was something I was still processing—*saved* my son. Granted, the piece of shit had merely freed my son, leaving my boy alone to fight against a half dozen fully transitioned werewolves. Still, he had given my son a fighting chance.

I said, "Not just your dad, baby. He's coming for you too."

"Why?"

"Remember how he helped you?"

Anthony snorted. "Some help. He just ripped the arrows out, meat and all. But I guess he did free me. He didn't actually, help, though. He left me to fight the werewolves alone."

"He did, yes. But the devil never does anything for free. He always, always wants something in return."

"Like what?"

"I don't know, baby."

"Mom, don't call me that."

"Sorry, baby. Oops."

I laughed, and so did he. We needed something to lighten the moment here. And as we laughed, something occurred to me, and it occurred to me in a flash of insight that I would ponder later: the devil had been created to fulfill a role. If he could be created, he could also be destroyed, too. The problem, of course, was that he could body-jump. I had come across such an entity before in the Pacific Northwest.

To destroy him, I had to destroy not his current body, which was only fleeting, but the source body. The original body. I nodded at that. Yes, find the devil's home base, and you found the source of evil. Kill the base, and you killed the devil—

Anthony's door opened. Standing in the doorway was Tammy, staring at me.

"Mom, her eyes," said Anthony.

I saw it too. The flames had grown, lapping just behind her pupils.

"The world needs the devil, Mom," she said, almost automatically. "You cannot know the light without the dark. Sound familiar?"

"He wants to use you. He wants to use Anthony too. If the devil had his way, he would take both of you from me."

"No one can use me, Mom," said Anthony. "No way, no how."

"You see, Mom," said Tammy. "No one will be using us. They can maybe try but they won't succeed."

"Baby, you do realize we're talking about the devil," I said, and heard myself all over again. The devil? Really?

"Yes, Mom. Yes, the devil. And, yes, your life is much different than it was ten years ago. All of our lives are. All because of you. Do you think I want to be a freak? Do you think Anthony likes being a freak? The kid has no friends. None, Mom."

"Hey, I have some—"

"And the friends I have all think I'm weird. Look at the burden I have. Every day I listen to stories of self-doubt, self-hate, of running away, of disappearing, of suicide, of hurting themselves and others. Every day. And all because of you."

"Baby, you know I didn't have control over what happened to me—"

"I know that, Mom," Tammy said. "But *you* decided to stay around. *You* decided to raise us normally. Except there was no normal, not any-more. Dad knew that. He knew you would hurt us in the end. And look at all the trouble you caused us. Anthony is a walking freak show—"

"Hey—"

I said, "That's not nice—"

"No, it's not nice," said Tammy, cutting me off. "It's a terrible thing to say about your little brother. A brother who could beat up a dozen men at once—"

"Well, it was like four. Maybe five—" Anthony said.

"A son who can turn into a goddamn monster—"

"That's enough, young lady—"

"The fire warrior isn't a monster," said Anthony. "He's a warrior. It's in his name. Duh."

"A name you gave him, dumbass."

"You will go to your room, young lady—"

"You know I'm right. And you know that you have been selfish by staying around. You know that we would have been better off if you had run away. Far away. I wouldn't be what I am. And Anthony would be—"

"Dead," said her little brother. "I would be dead."

"Or so Mom says. We have to take her word for it, don't we? The doctors might have saved you. You were at St. Jude's, the best children's hospital in the world."

Except I knew my daughter could see what I had seen in those dark hours. The black halo of death around my son. He had been on the brink of death, and she knew it. But was there a sliver of truth to what she said? Could he have survived and I unnecessarily and irrevocably altered my son's life?

"The answer is yes, Mom. You are selfish and terrible, and you are the real monster here." And with that, she marched out and slammed the bedroom door. Then slammed her door too.

Anthony looked at me and whistled. "Bitches be crazy."

24.

After chastising Anthony for calling his sister a bitch—and implying that all women were bitches—I called Kingsley and asked him to come over. Kingsley reminded me that he was a very important defense attorney with many high-stakes cases pending. I reminded him what we'd done a few nights ago, in bed. He said he would be right over.

Kingsley was with them now, and she wasn't very happy about it. Kingsley arrived bearing pizzas. Lots and lots of pizzas. Enough for ten people. Hell, twenty people. I made the boys promise to save a slice or two for Tammy. She still wasn't talking to me, and that was fine. I wasn't sure I wanted to talk to her either, not right now, not after her outburst.

Besides, she had given me a lot to think about.

Which is exactly what I had done, high overhead. In fact, I spent the rest of the evening flying and thinking and mulling over just about every decision I'd ever made. Talos listened and offered advice, and in the end, I knew I had to accept responsibility for everything. Maybe not for my initial attack, but everything after that.

Talos reminded me that I needed to be easy on myself and that I had done the best I could, under the circumstances, and I thanked my flying friend, but, ultimately, I knew Tammy was right. I had been selfish, and I had put everyone in harm's way. I liked to believe that I had also been loving and kind and helpful, that I had been there for them in ways that other mothers couldn't, but that didn't stop the burden of guilt from weighing me down and making me feel like shit all over again.

I flew and I flew and I might have kept on flying—and giving my daughter her wish—except I still had a job to do, and it was almost midnight.

***

I dropped down on Charlie Reed's roof, alighting quieter than most people would believe. There, I saw myself in the single flame—a rare chance for me to actually see myself from head to toe—and immediately transitioned from something big and scary, to something cute and maybe a little scary.

I'd carried with me a small tote bag with my

essentials: rolled jeans and sweater, Asics, wallet and my phone. No bra and no panties. I was changing on his rooftop, for crissakes. Who had time for all that? Besides, I'd been blessed—or cursed, depending on who you asked—with a small chest, which only seemed to have shrunk in my immortality. They don't tell you *that* in all those vampire romance books.

In two shakes of a lamb's tail, as my mother would say, I was dressed and dropping down from the roof. That it was two stories high mattered not at all. I landed easily, my knees painlessly absorbing the drop. I stumbled maybe only a fraction. Good enough.

Charlie had cameras all around his place, hence the reason I'd dressed on his roof. Had Charlie cared to really study my image, he might have noticed I was missing ears, or part of my neck, wherever the make-up foundation had failed to reach. So far, cameras hadn't been an issue with me, although there were undoubtedly hundreds of hours of strange security footage of vampires the world over, me included.

Although Allison possessed the kind of magic that Criss Angel could only dream of, she was still only human with mostly human limitations, hearing included. As yet, she hadn't realized I was coming up behind her. She stood on a wide, lighted footpath that led from the driveway to the front door. As I approached, she checked her phone, then scanned the street, then checked her phone again. She repeated this again and again.

I crept closer, noting the smooth sweep of her neck. Most vampires would find the smooth sweep of her neck irresistible; however, most vampires didn't have their inner demon under some semblance of control. I'm proud to say that I did. Mostly.

I crept closer, then closer still.

She was just about to check her cell phone again when I seized her shoulders, and said, *"I vant to suck your blood!"* in my best Boris Karloff impression.

Except I had barely gotten the words out when I found myself flying through the air. And then slamming hard into Charlie Reed's front door. What little air I had burst from my lungs as I slumped to my rump. Strange electrical currents crackled over my skin like living glow worms. I thought my hair was smoking.

"Oh my God, Sam! Are you okay?"

"I think I'm dying, Allison. Tell my children I love them. Tell Kingsley I will miss him, but not so much his hairy back. That I won't miss."

"Such a bitch. I could have hurt you."

I stood, dusted myself off. "You did hurt me."

"Why are you so mean to me?"

"I'm the one that got blasted."

"Serves you right."

"He's coming," I said.

"You're still smoking, Sam."

"Well, blow on me or something," I said.

Which is what she was doing when the front door opened and Charlie Reed appeared. "Now there's a sight you don't see every day," said Charlie Reed. "Come on in."

We followed him back through his spacious home, as Allison occasionally blew on my neck or hair. I smelled the burning too. There was a small chance one of her electrified worms had ignited my hair. Once in his office, he headed straight to his seat behind his desk.

"How's the writer's block?" I asked.

"Don't ask him that," hissed Allison. "That's, you know, taboo to ask a writer."

"I don't think it is," I said.

"I'm pretty sure it is, Sam."

"Well, it doesn't matter," said Charlie. "I've been doing nothing but staring at my screen for hours, ever since I got home from work. So I guess you can say the writer's block is going strong." He gave us an enthusiastic and sarcastic double thumbs-up.

Although we had both been hoping to read up a little more on the Land of Dur while we waited for Queen Autumn's possible midnight arrival, I suspected that the whole reason we were here in the first place was precisely because of his writer's block.

Allison caught my eye and nodded; indeed, we had discussed this earlier.

"Now?" she asked.

"Now," I said.

"Now what?" asked Charlie.

Allison and I both came around his desk and pulled up some extra chairs. I said, "Charlie, we need to talk."

***

And talk we did.

We laid on him some pretty heavy stuff. It's not every day that someone is told they are a creator, that the imaginings in his mind had sprung whole cloth into living, breathing people. More so, that an entire world had been created to support these people and creatures.

When Allison and I were done, he looked at us sadly. "Are you two okay? I mean, seriously."

"We are," I said. "Well, I am. I can't vouch for Allison."

"I'm fine, too," she snapped.

"Obviously, you two are pulling my leg," he said. He was sitting back in his office chair now, arms folded over his narrow chest, hair about as wild and unkempt as hair could be; I mean, had he looked in a mirror recently? Still, through it all, he was good looking. Bedraggled and messy, there was still no escaping that jawline. It was, I noted, thirty minutes before midnight.

"It would be the obvious answer," I said.

"That, or you two are crazy."

Allison and I had assumed he would balk at the suggestion he was a creator, that he had inadvertently created whole lives, both animal and man, and an entire whole world to populate them on. Truth was, I wasn't entirely convinced myself, although it felt right to me, too. Either way, he needed to wrap his brain around it in his own time, in his own way.

"Sam, I'm sorry, but that's impossible. I just hired you to investigate a haunting—"

"You've seen her, Charlie," I said. "Kind of."

He opened his mouth to speak but then closed it again, as, I assume, the real possibility that one of his characters might have come to life, truly occurred to him for the first time. "I-I never got a good look at her."

"It's Autumn," said Allison, jumping in. "And she's here for help."

"That's just crazy, Allie." He held up the phone bill. "I mean, yes, this is an uncannily accurate representation of the woman I see in my mind, but that still doesn't mean she's showing up here in my hallway." He paused, looked at me. "Perhaps the stress of this job has been too—"

"The stress of hanging out with my new favorite writer. The stress of relaxing in his beautiful home? The stress of meeting one of my favorite new characters, as well?"

"Well, maybe I misspoke. Perhaps the stress of

your job, in general, is affecting your—"

"Sorry, Charlie. You're my only client." Which was sad but true. Unless one works in a big firm— and Moon Investigations, to be clear, is not a big firm—a private eye generally works one case at a time. Although we may get lucky and a few might overlap, there are usually whole days, sometimes whole weeks, where I wait for work.

"Maybe this job finally pushed you over the edge," he suggested.

"Maybe," I said. "Except you know there's a chance we might be right."

"Just to be clear," said Allison. "The stress of my job hasn't been too much for me, either." We both looked at her, and she sort of sank back into the couch. "Just saying," she mumbled. "But no one asked me, of course."

"How long have you been thinking of the world of Dur?" I asked Charlie after we both ignored Allison.

"Nearly my entire life. My earliest notes on it were when I was eight."

"And you're, what? Thirty-five?"

"Forty-four. And thanks. Still, that proves—"

"You've been living in this World of Dur for more than thirty years," I cut in.

"Well, yes. But not really living..." But he thought about, then retracted. "Okay, maybe I have daydreamed about it. Perhaps even often."

"How often?" asked Allison.

"Usually throughout most days. Maybe before I go to sleep. Maybe when I wake up. In the shower. In the hot tub. Sometimes when I'm jogging and often when I'm walking."

"That's nearly every waking minute," pointed out Allison.

"Well, not when I work. My job is tough."

"Let me guess," I said. "But you find yourself thinking about it on breaks and lunch, and on your drive to and from work?"

He shrugged, crossed his arms over his chest. "Well, yeah. But most writers probably do the same thing, right?"

"I would question that," I said. "I would question the sheer amount of thought you put into your world compared to other writers. I am sure they have only thought of their own stories a mere fragment compared to—"

"What about J.R.R. Tolkien?" he said suddenly. "Or J.K. Rowling?"

I let his question sink in, as he had just listed the two authors who, I suspected, were also very much creators. Two authors known for having made extensive notes on their worlds. Whole volumes of Middle Earth history existed. And J.K. Rowling herself had created a veritable gallery of drawing of all her characters, each rendered lovingly and exquisitely. As if... well, as if she had been doing an actual portrait of an actual living, breathing man, woman, or magical creature.

"I assume I'm only buttressing your point," he finally said, sinking back into his chair.

"You are," I said. "And no one uses buttressing in the real world."

"What's a butt dress?" asked Allison.

"See?" I said.

"Be that as it may," said Charlie, "I refuse to join your crazy little party. I think, maybe, we should call this your last night."

"We could," I said. "And we'll leave right now if you think that's best. But know this, until you get past your writer's block, your ghost is going to keep showing up, right there in that hallway. Looking for help. From you, her creator. C'mon, Allison. Let's go."

My friend didn't like it, but she understood a standoff when she saw one. She extricated herself from the couch and stood with me.

I said to Charlie, "I'll email you my final bill. Also, could you please let us know when the final book is published?"

"Sure," he said glumly. His hands were crossed in his lap and his head was bowed. He looked like he could have been praying to his own creator. "Except I haven't written in four months, ever since my wife left me."

"I know," I said. I waited. I also waited for him to make the connection. On his own. He didn't. Not yet.

I touched Allison's shoulder. "C'mon."

We were just exiting the study when his voice reached us. "The ghost appeared not long after."

I paused, waited. Allison took my hand. I let her.

"Except she's not a ghost, is she?" Now I heard the wonder in his voice. The sheer, beautiful, infectious, earth-shaking wonder. "It's Queen Autumn. And she needs my help. Son of a bitch."

25.

We waited. He needed to work through this. The weight on him, I suspected, was enormous. I kept the option of erasing his memory of it on the table. At least, the memory of this last day.

"So they're *all* real?" he said again. He ran his fingers through his unkempt hair, making it more unkempt. I think once or twice he fought back a little vomit. After all, in his world, there had been much death and destruction as well.

"I think so," I said. It was now twenty minutes before midnight.

"Had I known, I would never have..." his voice trailed off. "I would never have killed off any of them. Or hurt any of them."

"I know," I said. "But they also wouldn't have been alive either."

"What do you mean?"

"You loved them," I said. "Even the terrible characters. Even the monsters. You loved them all, with all your heart, for decades. They were real people, with real motivations, both good and bad. Sometimes good and bad people get hurt or killed."

"Then I shouldn't have loved them, or even wanted to tell their story!"

"Then you wouldn't have been alive, either," said Allison. "Their stories, their world, their hopes and dreams, gave you life too."

"Please tell me I'm dreaming," he said, burying his face in his hands. "Please tell me this isn't real."

Allison and I looked at each other. Neither of us knew what to do. I had never met a creator, and I especially had never been around one who just discovered that his creations were, in fact, real. Admittedly, it was hard to watch. He stood and paced, he cursed God and the heavens, he buried his face in his hands and wept. Sometimes he just stood there and laughed, nearly hysterically. Once or twice he hugged himself. All while the clock marched inevitably toward midnight.

With a few minutes to go, he finally collapsed between us on the couch again, where Allison and I had sat. I could smell the sweat on him now. I could also see some semblance of acceptance in his eyes.

He looked at me. "What do I do?"

"I don't know," I said.

"I haven't written in four months," he said.

"I know."

"Is that why Autumn…" He paused, and I secretly wondered if he loved her most of all. "Is that why Autumn is here? Her baby?"

"I think so."

"But I don't understand. Is their world on..." He paused again, searching for the right word. "On hold?"

Allison and I had thought about that, and had concluded that we didn't know. We said as much to Charlie.

"Their world just *stopped?*" he said, standing again, pacing again, running his hands through his hair again. I could see the mad genius flashing in his 'yes.' I could see his mind going in a hundred directions at once. Mostly, I could feel his sheer passion and love for what he had created. His sympathy and knowing. He knew all of them, down to every last person. Like a true god. There was, after all, decades of momentum here. This wasn't a man who decided to write just a few months ago, or even a few years ago. This was a man who had lived in this world for nearly all his life. I was, quite simply, watching a creator create.

"Yes, yes," he said, pacing faster, his eyes flashing with light in a way that hinted at the super-natural. "When I stopped writing, they stopped living. But not really. No, not really, because I think about them continuously, often, and wonder what they are up to. But their lives, for the most part, are on hold. They are waiting for me to finish this tale."

"And to start new ones," said Allison, sounding, suddenly, every bit the fangirl that she was. That we both were. I wouldn't have minded if Charlie wrote a hundred more stories set in the World of Dur. That is, before I knew their lives were real. Would it make reading the book different, knowing that people were really living and really dying? Really suffering and really loving, too? I didn't know, but it was an... exciting prospect. I caught Allison's eye, and she nodded with me, having followed my train of thought.

"There's one problem," said Charlie, and slumped down next to us again.

"Writer's block," I said.

He nodded glumly.

Allison said, "Have you ever had writer's block before?"

"Well, I've never really written before. This is my first book. Everything I've done up to this point was daydreaming and note taking. I have hundreds of notepads filled with character sketches and notes and histories of Dur."

I said, "And when you started writing, you were consumed with the book?"

"Oh, yes."

"And your wife thought she had lost you."

"I wouldn't come up for air for days. I used up all my vacation time and called in sick constantly. It was all I could talk about or think about. I got to work late, and left early."

"Until they fired you," I said.

"Yes."

"And your wife had finally had enough," said Allison.

He nodded. "Yes."

I said, "And in one fell swoop, you lost your wife and your job was in jeopardy..."

"And any day now my house," he added.

I said, "Which all adds up to one hell of a case of writer's block."

He looked at us, nodded. Sweat was on his brow. "I gave up everything for my writing, and now I can't write either, all while the very world I created suffers. I am in hell."

If anything, we might have made his writer's block worse.

Allison nodded, picking up my thought. She reached out and took one of Charlie's fidgeting hands. He stopped fidgeting and his hand closed around hers. He held onto her as if she were a lifeline. I suspected he was drowning in his own way.

In that moment, a bluish glow appeared in the hallway. I glanced at my cell phone and was not surprised to see that it was midnight.

"She's here," I said.

"Autumn?" asked Charlie, snapping his head up.

"Yes."

26.

I moved over to the hallway opening, slowly, so as to not scare Autumn. Then again, I seriously doubted she could see me. Neither Allison nor Charlie could see her, and Charlie had created her. Except that Allison could see what I saw, by dipping into my mind.

"Is she there?" asked Charlie. He had come up behind me too. He was turning his head this way and that, trying to catch a glimpse of her in his peripheral vision. Apparently, sometimes he could, and sometimes he couldn't. His human eyes, quite simply, were not used to seeing into the super-natural.

"Yes," I said.

The closer we got to the hallway, the more Queen Autumn seemed to fidget. She held her hands up like a mime, pushing against an invisible wall. In fact, she seemed to be doing the "trapped-in-a-box routine," as she now pushed against either side of her too. Except, she really seemed to be pushing against something... invisible.

Was the queen a mime, too? asked Allison.

No. She's inspecting something, searching for something.

For what?

I don't know.

Now, the queen cocked her head to one side, as if listening. After a moment of this, she bent down and inspected the floor, then stood up on her toes and felt above her, as if on an unseen shelf. She wore a loose gown that I suspected were pajamas in her world. Either way, they looked cozy as hell.

"What's she doing, Sam?" asked Charlie.

We were all standing before the hallway archway by now. Autumn was there, looking directly at us, but not really. Sometimes she made direct eye contact with me but that was only in passing. It was obvious that she couldn't see us, but I suspected she could *sense* us. After all, I could see the confusion, the strain, the eagerness and the hope on her face. Her mouth moved as well, although I couldn't make out any words.

"She knows we're here," I said.

Allison, who had been filling my head with her own presence, was seeing what I was seeing in real time. She said, "Sam, she appears to be in a closet of some sort."

"A wardrobe," said Charlie suddenly, and I realized how nice it was to have the actual creator of the world next to us, even if he did seem a bit confused. "And it's not just any wardrobe."

"Is there a lion and witch in it?" asked Allison.

"Not quite," said Charlie. His breath smelled vaguely of coffee. I wondered if all writers' breath smelled of coffee. "The wardrobe hasn't made it into the novel yet, but it's there, in my notes."

"What kind of wardrobe is it?" I asked.

"It's how Queen Autumn communicates with..." but his voice trailed off.

"Communicates with who?" I asked, although I could have just as easily found the answer in his thoughts.

His voice sounded distant and hollow when he said, "With God."

***

I looked at Allison; she looked at me.

Charlie stepped lithely between us, and reached out a hand toward the shimmering doorway. At least, it was shimmering to my eyes.

"As queen, midnight is typically the only time she has to herself," said Charlie, lowering his hand. "But when her husband sleeps, and most of the castle has quieted, she slips out of bed and some-times opens her wardrobe, to speak to God."

"You mean to you," said Allison.

Charlie didn't turn around, but he gave us a full view of his strong profile, his sharp nose, squarish jaw. "I never imagined the door would lead here, to my hallway."

"You are her creator," said Allison.

He said nothing, although that jawline might have rippled.

I said, "But the scene never made it into the book. How would she know about the wardrobe?"

Charlie was shaking his head before I had a chance to finish the question. "The closet has been known to her family for centuries. She knew about it at an early age, consulted it often. It just didn't make it into the first book, yet."

"So your characters can live outside the first book?" asked Allison.

"Of course," he said. "Their lives extend well beyond the pages."

"Except for this story," I said. "Maybe their lives are on hold, or perhaps aspects of their lives."

"Maybe," said Charlie.

"Like maybe the queen's daughter is still kidnapped until Charlie resolves it!" said Allison.

It sounded crazy, but it also seemed plausible. Charlie stood for a long moment, staring forward, while Queen Autumn stood just before him, searching, as well. She reached out a hand, but it faded away before it could find us.

"You said her family has been speaking to God

for centuries," said Allison. "But she's only recently come to your house, to this hallway."

Charlie was shaking his head again. "They *believe* they are talking to God. They never, in fact, found God."

"Until now," I said.

Charlie's shoulders rolled up, and seemed, in general, uncomfortable with this whole conversation. Finally, he said, "Queen Autumn was different. She always believed she would find him."

"In the wardrobe?" asked Allison.

"Yes, at first," said Charlie. "And then later, in her heart."

I nodded, recalling her devotion from even at an early age, even if it had been barely hinted at in the novel. I said, "She senses you're near."

In the book, just where Charlie had left the story hanging, Queen Autumn had awakened to discover that her newborn was missing, kidnapped in the night. Charlie had set the stage for a mystery within the greater novel.

But his characters never stopped living, I thought, and watched Autumn's beautiful blue eyes searching and searching, her hands reaching out, her lips moving in what I assumed was a prayer.

"Do you hear her?" I asked Charlie, for he had stepped closer still, cocking his head, listening. Creator and created were now mere inches from each other.

"I hear... something," he said, as some of the

shimmering blue light touched his skin, although he didn't seem to notice it.

"Is it also midnight in the land of Dur?" asked Allison.

Charlie, who had raised a hand and placed it just inside the blue light, said, "Since I never established time zones, I would imagine their time defaulted to our own time."

I shrugged. It made sense.

Allison was about to ask another nonsensical question—

Hey! came her hurt thought.

—when I shushed her. After all, Queen Autumn had raised her own hand as well. I watched with some interest as his hand and her hand found each other's, but not really. I doubted he could see her; at least, not yet. Maybe he would in time, but I didn't know.

"I-I feel her, I think," he said.

Opposite him, Autumn covered her mouth with her other hand. Tears flowed freely down her face.

"She feels you too," I said.

"She's weeping," he said.

"Yes," I said.

"Now... she's asking for help. She's asking for my help to save her baby."

He stood there for another heartbeat or two, then pulled his hand back, breaking the connection. Tears streamed down his face as well.

"What's happening, Sam?" he asked.

At this point, I figured it was a rhetorical question. I said, "Something beautiful."

In the hallway, Autumn sank to her knees and she covered her face with both hands, weeping, her body quaking, and my heart went out to her. After all, I had come to love her and her world and her whole crazy family. Oh, and her hunky First Knight. I loved them all, even the bad boys.

Charlie said, "But I can't help her, Sam. I can't help any of them. I-I can't write. I've forgotten how. Or it's left me. Or something's wrong with me. I don't know what to do to help her. Please, Sam. You have to help me. Please." He sank into his couch, covered his own face.

"Maybe we can help her," I said.

"What do you mean?" asked Charlie, peeking through his fingers.

Allison shot me a look, no doubt picking up my thoughts. "You can't be serious, Sam."

"Oh, but I am," I said to her, and to Charlie, I said, "Write us into the story."

***

"Okay, now that's just crazy talk," said Charlie.

"No crazier than any of it," I said.

"And what's with this 'writing *us* into the story' business?" asked Allison.

"You know you would give your left pinkie to visit the World of Dur, for real."

Allison thought about, while Charlie looked from one to the other of us, the expression on his face suggesting that we had all gone mad.

"Okay, maybe just the tip," said Allison.

"You two are serious," he said.

"She needs help, Charlie," I said, looking again at the queen, who was still weeping in her hands. Not too long ago, my own son had been kidnapped. Not fun at all. "And she needs help now," I added.

"But I haven't written a stitch in months. And also, this is complete lunacy."

I ignored him. "We know where her baby is being held. We followed the kidnapper closely in Chapter Thirteen, your last chapter."

"Hold on," said Charlie.

"For what?" I asked.

Charlie fished out his cell phone. "I'm calling the local funny farm. Tell them they have three new patients."

I said, "Instead of cracking jokes, I need you to find it within yourself to write a couple of sentences in the next chapter—"

"Sam, you don't know what you are asking. I can't—"

"I need you to buckle down and do this one thing."

"Sam..." and he looked from me to his desk, and I saw the sweat on his brow. "That story has caused a lot of upheaval in my life."

"And you've caused a lot of upheaval in her

life," I said, jabbing a thumb in the general vicinity of the glowing hallway behind me.

"Sam, I don't know what you want from me..."

"I want you to write two or three sentences, tops."

"And what will these sentences say?"

I thought about that. I wasn't a writer. I was barely a texter. Hell, most of my texts were riddled with misspellings. Once, not long ago, I tried posting something on Facebook, and edited what had been once been a page down to just a few sentences. Then deleted it altogether. No, I wasn't a writer, but Charlie was, and he needed to wake up.

Allison jumped in. "Then just make a few notes. You said it yourself, the wardrobe isn't even in the book yet."

I looked at him. "We need just a few lines of notes. Can you do it?"

"I... I don't know. What is it you are asking?"

"Write us into your book. At least, into your notes."

"Wait," said Allie. "What's to stop him from making us a recurring character or something? What if we can never leave?"

I said, "Charlie can't control when we come and go. He can only open a doorway. It's our decision whether or not we accept the invitation. And our decision when we return."

"You seem to know a lot about something that we all have just barely been introduced to..."

Charlie began, but trailed off when I gave him a small suggestion that I knew what I was talking about and that he should let it go. He nodded.

"Sam, can I talk to you?" said Allison, and we ducked out of the office, leaving Charlie to stand before the glowing archway, scratching his head.

Once in another of many hallways, Allison spun me around. "But do you, Sam? Do you really know what you are talking about?"

"Kinda sorta," I said.

"Kinda sorta doesn't keep me from being trapped in the World of Dur for the rest of my life, as appealing as that might sound, or even get us there in the first place."

"The world is real, Allie. You can see that. It's just a matter of getting us there."

"Well, can't you do your flame thingy?"

"I could, but it won't work."

"How do you know it won't work?"

"His world is exclusive," I said.

"Exclusive?"

"Invite only."

"So he really does have to write us in?"

"He does."

"And you know this how? Never mind. Talos," she said, reading my mind.

"I had a talk with him on the way over," I said.

"Fine," said Allison. "But I want to go on record that this is your hare-brained idea."

"Duly noted," I said.

We found Charlie pacing before the arched opening into the hallway, within which I could see Autumn on her knees, her head bowed, perhaps in prayer. He looked at us when we came in. "I dunno, you two. If this is real, and it's maybe, maybe looking like it is, I can't in good conscience send you to my world. It's a very dangerous world."

"We can handle ourselves," I said, and gave him another suggestion to believe that we were very capable women who, in fact, could very much handle ourselves.

"I believe you," he said. "But in what capacity do I write you in? I mean, I can't just have two women from Earth show up in my world."

He ran his fingers through his hair, grabbed hold of it and really pulled. Ouch.

Allison jumped in. "She's in there praying now, right?" she asked, looking at me.

"Yes," said Charlie. "I can hear her. My God, I can hear her."

"Well, what if her prayers are answered?"

"What do you mean?" he asked, stopping before her.

Allison looked at me. "That's all I had."

I jumped in. "What if two angels appear, sent from God, in answer to her prayers?"

"Two angels?"

"Yes."

Charlie was lost in thought. Either that, or he was having a very inappropriate fantasy. "Yes," he said. "Even better, I can leave the two new characters—you and Allison—undefined, and allow Queen Autumn to decide what they—you—are."

"There you go," I said.

"Now, you just need to write us into your notes," said Allie. "Do you think you can do that much?"

"I-I think so, yes."

"And can you do it now," I said. "The queen needs our help."

Charlie nodded, then nodded a little more vigorously. "Yes, by God. I can at least do that!" He hustled around his too-big desk and settled in. He cracked his neck and fingers. His computer fired up.

I turned and looked through the archway, through the blue glow. On bended knee, Autumn now lay nearly prostate before us on in the floor, her hands before us, her hair splayed around her like something drifting on the surface of water.

When the computer was up and running, and when Charlie had cracked every conceivable knuckle on his body—including, I think, his toes—and with Allison and I standing near the hallway entrance, Charlie took in a deep breath, and began typing...

It didn't take long at all for me to sense a change in the hallway.

Despite myself, I gasped. A second or two later, Allison gasped, too.

27.

"Sam, are you seeing what I'm seeing?" Allison asked.

"I think so," I said.

"Seeing what?" asked Charlie, pushing away from his desk and coming around to stand with us. "Did it work?"

"Yes," I said.

"Very much so," said Allison.

"Well, I still don't see anything."

Indeed, the shimmering blue light was gone. So, too, was the ghost-like form of Queen Autumn. In her place was a very real-looking version of the new royal mother, as she bowed before us, deep in prayer. I knew it was prayer, because I could hear her quite clearly now.

"She speaks English?" asked Allison.

"Not quite," said Charlie. "But for the sake of the story, her language is automatically translated into English. Which is probably why you can understand her. You can really see her?"

"I can, yes."

"Why can't I see her?" he asked.

"Because you haven't written yourself into the story," I said.

"I'm... I'm not sure I am prepared to do that," he said.

"You don't have to," I said. "You can keep the barrier between you and them."

"But that won't stop them from seeking you," said Allison. "Like Queen Autumn."

"Can she see you?" he asked.

"Hard to say. She's bowed down, but she would have heard us by now, I think."

"Why can't she see you?"

I thought about that. "Because this is *our* entry point into *her* world," I said. "Not the other way around."

He shrugged. "Fine. So what now?"

I looked at Allison; she looked at me. She took my hand again, and I was not very surprised to feel hers was sweating a little. I looked into the hallway, at the still-prostrate queen. "We go in," I said.

"Wait," said Allie, and she took a few deep breaths and placed her hand over her heart.

"What are you doing?" I asked.

"A prayer to Mother Earth to anchor us." She

pointed down. "Look."

I was surprised to discover that a tiny silver cord that had appeared somewhere in the vicinity of my navel. It dropped down through the Spanish tile floor.

"It goes all the way to Mother Earth's heart, Sam. Now, we can never get lost. We need only to follow the cord home."

"Oh broth..." I began, and nearly rolled my eyes, but then saw the brilliance of her plan. "Actually, good thinking."

"Nice catch, Sam. And thank you."

"Are you ready?" I asked.

"I am," she said. "Should we leave our cell phones behind?"

"Why?" I asked.

"I dunno. Maybe they would be viewed as a kind of witchcraft."

"She does have a point," said Charlie.

"Fine," I said, and we tossed our phones on a nearby end table.

Once done, I looked back at Charlie, who seemed pained and anxious, then looked at Allison, who nodded. Together, we stepped through the archway.

28.

The passing from one reality to another was not unlike teleporting.

A small disorientation, followed by a stumble or two, and then a lot of blinking and taking it all in. And what I took in was nothing short of a dank, smallish room, composed entirely of massive, fitted rocks, with only a small, square window in the upper half of the room, from which pale light filtered through. The room itself was dark, but my eyes were alive and well, seeing the smaller light that wriggled through the air, and illuminated everything. Good to see my own skills had come through with me. Next to me, Allison held out her hand and a small ball of light appeared. She made another gesture and the light rose up and hovered near the ceiling, lighting up the place.

A gasp from the floor, and then a small scream.

After all, we were nearly standing on top of the stretched-out Queen Autumn, who was now sitting up on her knees and looking from one of us to the other. Lord, she was beautiful. And, yes, just a little off. Too beautiful. Eyes too round, cheeks too round, breasts too round. She was, no doubt, every man's dream. At least, Charlie's dream.

The queen, upon taking us in—including our strange garb—was about to let loose with another scream, and this one wasn't going to be small. It was gonna be huge and it was going to alert the guards that I knew, thanks to having read the book, were always stationed nearby. And since we couldn't have that, I was behind her in a blink, covering her mouth with my hand. My cold, cold hand, which caused her to shudder. *My life.*

"No screaming, Your Highness," I whispered into her ear. "We're here to help you find your baby."

I also gave her the most subtle of suggestions to trust us. The truth was, this was my first "other world" experience, and I was a little freaked out, too. Sure, I might switch bodies temporarily with Talos, and I might even be sitting quietly by his side in his own world, but my *mind* wasn't with my body, not yet, although Talos told me I could someday experience his world, too. Although I might have gotten fleeting glimpses of his world, I had never fully immersed myself in it.

You've been to other worlds, too, came Allison's thoughts. *The moon and Mars, remember?*

She was right, of course. Yes, I had tested the limits of my teleportation, and so far, there hadn't seemed to be any. Limits, that is. Still, this world felt different. It wasn't a barren planet or moon. It was real, and it was filled, I knew, with real characters with real hopes and dreams. Also real magic, and real monsters, too. A strange and thriving place. Yes, Charlie had quite the imagination.

Meanwhile, Queen Autumn was beginning to struggle in my hands, and, since I didn't want to hurt her, I gave her an even stronger suggestion to settle down. I telepathically asked if she understood me, and she nodded. I did not want trouble in a strange world. I mean, no more than was necessary. After all, I kinda liked Earth. And my kids. And Kingsley.

And...?

And you, too, Allie.

I sighed and carefully released my hand from the queen's mouth. After all, I wasn't sure if my telepathic suggestions would stick in this new world. Alas, she looked frightened but didn't scream.

So far, so good.

I stepped around the queen and held out a hand. She stared at me as if she were seeing a ghost. How's that for irony? Finally, she took it and I helped her to her slippered feet. She towered a good eight inches over me, which put her at damn near six feet tall.

"Who art thou?" she asked. She spoke with a lilting accent to her words, and I wondered if Charlie had unwittingly imagined characters with a slight British accent. She hid the fear in her voice; she was a strong woman.

I considered her question. Should I tell her my real name? Would any of this, somehow, make it into the novel? I wasn't sure what would be written, and what would be considered "behind the scenes." After all, in the novel, her baby had very much been kidnapped, and the reader was left heartbroken. I know I sure was. I felt the queen's pain, perhaps more so than most. Obviously, we were already in his notes, and thus a part of the fabric of his world.

Still, I thought it best to give her a fake name. I said, "I'm Lady Tam Tam, and this is my servant girl, Allie the Wench." I might have grinned.

"I see," said Queen Autumn. "And from where doth thou hail, Lady Tam Tam?"

"I haileth frometh—"

Too much, Sam, thought Allie.

I tried again. "We hail from the County of Oranges," I said.

"The County of Oranges?" she said. "And where is this county? I have not heard of such a place."

"It is nestled along the western shores, Your Highness. Famous for its beaches, babes, and plastic surgeons."

Sam! hissed Allie in my mind.

"Plastic surgeons?" asked the queen.

"It is a special type of wizard, Your Highness, trained in the dark arts of reducing age and enlarging breasts."

"Mayhap I would like to visit such a surgeon. I have surely aged a decade or two in these past few weeks alone."

"Weeks?" I asked, confused.

"Yes. Two weeks ago to this day, my baby girl was taken from me."

I considered. What had been two weeks for her, was four months for us, since Charlie had last put pen to paper, as the writers of old used to say. Then again, it would make sense that her world hadn't kept pace with our world. Why should it? Charlie could sit down and simply start the story where he had left off, with no time elapsing in their world at all.

I said to the queen, "It is why we are here, Your Highness."

She put a hand to her chest. "I do not understand."

I took in some air, and noted it was clean and fresh and no doubt suffused with the right amount of oxygen. A good thing because otherwise, Allison wouldn't have made it this far. She glanced at me and nodded. It hadn't occurred to me to worry about such a thing, but it had worried Allison. Of course, I wouldn't have known it worried Allison, since she kept me blocked from her thoughts these days.

Focus, Sam, she intoned in my thoughts.

I nodded, released the breath, looked straight into Queen Autumn's beautiful eyes, and said, "God has heard your prayers, Your Highness. And He sent us to help."

29.

She stared at us.

We were certainly stare-worthy. I was dressed in a black tee-shirt with the words: "Think Pink" scrawled in pseudo-lipstick across the chest. My distressed jeans had stylish tears in the knees. Viewed from her regal perspective, they undoubtedly looked anything but stylish. My sneakers glittered with silver and were as cute as cute could be. But to a princess, they might have looked, well, enchanted.

Allison was dressed in an unbuttoned maroon flannel shirt, with a black tank top underneath. Her jeans were black, as were her silver-tipped black boots. Allison tended to dress a bit bleaker—

Insert stylish, came her words.

—than me. One would think she was the

vampire and I was the nerdy telephone hotline psychic.

Hey!

Ignoring Allison, I said to the queen, "We dress unusually in the County of Oranges."

"I would say so. Although, I do find your attire rather intriguing. Mayhap I could try on a pair of similar trousers?"

"Er, mayhap," I said, and wondered if Charlie could write in a village Gap store. Le Gappe Shoppe?

"And you are really here in answer to my prayers?"

"Yes, Your Highness."

"And the Good Lord sent you?"

"Yes, Your Highness."

"All the way from the County of Oranges?"

"Yes, Your Highness."

"And you heard the Lord's call?"

"We did, yes."

Her eyes narrowed. "You are close to the Lord?"

"I am, in a way."

"You are a sort of priestess then?"

I did my best to remember if this land approved of priestesses or not, but couldn't remember. "In the sense that I have direct communication with the Creator, then, yes, you could say that I'm a priestess."

She nodded. "And how did you get past the

guards?"

I glanced at the open wardrobe, which, from this side of the room, looked far more intricate and immaculate than I could have imagined.

She said, "You hailed from the wardrobe?"

"I did, Your Highness."

"Then you are from the Creator?"

"Like I said, he sent us in response to your prayers."

"To find my baby?"

"Yes, Your Highness."

She took in some air, and summoned an inner courage that I doubted even I could find within myself, in such a situation. "Then my fate, my life, my hope, my everything is in your hands."

I next did something that surprised even me, and sure as heck surprised her. I reached out and drew her in tight, and hugged her harder than I had any right to, but I didn't care. She sank into me almost immediately, and soon hot tears flowed down my neck.

It was a few minutes later before she stepped back, wiping her eyes. "You are cold, Lady Tam Tam."

"I am, yes."

"We need to warm you—"

"My kind is never warm, Your Highness."

"Do I want to know what manner of being you are?"

"Probably not."

"Very well. But you are here to save my baby?"

"We are," I said.

"Then we shouldn't delay a drammit longer."

Allison's words in my mind: *They are the equivalent of seconds, remember?*

I nodded, recalling. "I agree. Not a drammit longer."

"What do you need from me?" the queen asked.

Allison and I exchanged glances. We knew the story well; most important, we knew who kidnapped her baby. And where she was being held.

I said, "Lead us to the dungeon."

30.

It was late and the castle was quiet.

Guards stood at the head of each hallway and floor; all bowed deeply as we approached. Many kept their gaze on us, and one or two made to block us, until a snappy order from their queen got them to back off. The guards were tall and muscular. Most sported broadswords sheathed to their backs, and smaller rapiers hitched along their hips. The sentries all looked vaguely similar, and I wondered if this was a result of the limits of Charlie's imagination. Had he simply mentioned that all the castle guards were tall, muscular and square-jawed? I suspected he had. Which begged the question: was this world only as detailed as Charlie described? Or was it able to extend beyond even his imagination, and take on a life of its own, so to speak?

I didn't know, but judging by the sameness of the castle guards, I was beginning to suspect the answer lay somewhere with the former. Obviously, Charlie hadn't described each and every sentry's physical appearance in the book. That would have bogged down the book. Nor had he described every inch of these hallways, yet I could see the individual bricks that made up the walls. Anthony once described the process of how video games were made using texture-mapping, which was a method of repeating details throughout a game, with variances for lighting, weather, and other factors that the programmers had determined to be important.

Really, Sam? Video games? We have a baby to find.

Aren't you at all curious about how this world was actually made?

Not right now.

We turned another corner and headed down a flight of steep, circular stairs. According to Charlie, we were in the royal keep. I ran my hand along the wall, noting the solidity of it, and the general massiveness of the structure itself. And all from the mind of one man. No, one creator.

When the stairs leveled off, Queen Autumn led the way forward, her evening gown flowing behind her. The lolling guards, clearly surprised by her sudden late-night visit, snapped to attention—and then promptly reached for their swords when they saw us. She waved them all away. Surely the three of us were a curious sight.

We entered a massive hall lined with tapestries so ornate that Charlie must have spent considerable time on them in his notes, as I didn't recall them mentioned in the book. After all, he had spent a lifetime on those notes, having only recently put pen to paper for his first novel.

The tapestries were quickly forgotten—and so was all thought, for that matter—when I spied the man standing at the far end of the room. Both Allison and I gasped, recognizing the great knight immediately. Sir Rory, the queen's protector knight, was unlike anyone I had ever seen, and probably would never see again. In the book, Charlie had spent considerable time on the man, who undoubtedly filled many pages of notes, too. Unlike the cookie-cutter guards who filled the upper levels of the castle, this man was a shining beacon of detail: the long, flowing, white hair. The bare, broad shoulders. The leather jerkin must have seen dozens if not hundreds of battles. Leather trousers that were entirely too form-fitting for my own and Allison's own good. Boots that marched up his calves, laced with silver buckles. A long broadsword that ran diagonally from one shoulder down to the opposite hip. Only Kingsley would have matched the size and breadth of Sir Rory.

Rory stepped away from the young man he'd been conversing with—a man I immediately recognized by his unruly black hair as the knight-in-training, Caleb—and blocked our path. We all pulled up short, although I might not have minded running headlong into the big man standing before us. I imagined his cat-like reflexes would have kept me on my feet, all while he held me up with those strong arms.

Hey, said Allison, *I just had the same thought! Are you sure you can't read my mind?*

Never mind that, I thought. *You know what to do, right?*

I do, she replied, and, without breaking stride, Allison raised both hands and said something just under her breath. I knew her magic was earth-based magic, and often worked in concert with Gaia herself, Mother Earth. How this translated into another world, I didn't know, but I suspected she was calling upon the nature entities around her—nature entities in this world—seeking their help and guidance, and whatever else they could offer her.

"Stop, witch!" said Rory, and made to draw his sword, but I was behind him before he could, and I caught his reaching hand behind his back. I used some of my old agency training, and drove a knee into the back of one leg. And with nearly all my strength, I forced him down to his stomach and face, his arm still pinned behind him. In his defense, the movement had been faster than any he'd probably ever seen. That I had the great knight pinned to the ground was not something I was especially proud of. I knew Rory to be a good man and fearless warrior. Little did he know the depth of the betrayal around him.

As he struggled, and as the Queen stood back, aghast, a pulsing bubble of clear energy expanded from Allison's hands.

Squire Caleb leaped forward, drawing his own sword and swinging it so fast and smooth that I was certain I wasn't going to reach him in time before Allison got her head cut off. I had just made a move to stop him when the bubble of energy burst and Caleb and his sword somersaulted backward, only to be pinned against the domed ceiling high above.

Due to all the excitement, I had relaxed my hold on Rory, and the man sent me hurtling through the air. Unlike Caleb, I landed on my feet and turned and faced the realm's most decorated knight, who just so happened to be the queen's right-hand personal protector, a man she was secretly in love with, and he with her. Good stuff, all of which had kept me riveted to the pages.

"Stop!" shouted a voice. It was the queen, and, to her credit, she leaped between us, holding the hem of her gown.

"My Queen, they are witches—"

"They are angels, Sir Rory."

The man blinked. "I thought I heard you say *angels*, Your Highness."

"Indeed. They were sent from the Creator, Rory. You must trust me on this. They are here in answer to my prayers. They are here to find my baby."

"But they attacked the noble Caleb!"

"If I might interject here," I said, glancing at Allie. Her thin but muscular arms shook as she focused the energy that kept the squire pinned to the ceiling. "Squire Caleb isn't who you think he is. Squire Caleb has been dabbling in the dark arts."

"What are you saying, Lady Tam Tam?" asked the queen.

"Possession," said Rory, lowering his sword. He turned and stared up at the young man still pinned to the ceiling. "By Gods, that makes sense. The strange behavior. The strange questions. The strange... everything."

"Possessed by whom?" asked the queen.

"I think you know, Your Highness," I said.

"The Foul Wizard Xander?"

"Indeed," I said.

Queen Autumn turned to Allison. "Bring him down, Wench Allie."

My friend shot me an irritated look, then closed her eyes. Above, nearly invisible cords had appeared and looped around the young squire. Then Allie opened her eyes and lowered her hands, and as she did so, the young man, now rotating in the air like a rotisserie chicken, floated down.

"Impressive," I said under my breath.

"And don't you forget it, *Lady Tam Tam*," she hissed back.

The young man came to rest on his feet and probably would have stumbled and fallen if not for

Allison and her ability to control the energy around her.

Queen Autumn stood before the young man. "What have you to say for yourself?"

"He can't talk, Your Highness," said Allison, grunting a little. I suspected the Foul Wizard Xander was fighting her with a little magic of his own.

A lot of magic, she mentally grunted. *I can't hold him off for long.*

"Queen Autumn," I said, "Xander conspired to kidnap your daughter."

The squire's eyes widened manically. And just as the queen and Rory moved toward him, Caleb/Xander burst free from Allison's bonds. Opaque cords flew in every direction, only to dissolve before they hit the ground.

Caleb turned and faced Allison.

"This isn't the last you've seen of me, witch!"

"I knew it!" said Rory, looking at us.

And with that, Caleb spun once, twice, and three times for good measure, and disappeared from the room.

"Merciful Mother of us all," whispered the queen.

I kind of had to agree.

31.

With our little confrontation having garnered the attention of nearly the entire castle, Rory ordered everyone out of the great hall, except for the queen and us.

Now, the great warrior paced before us, keeping a hand on his hilt. I noted his broad shoulders and little butt. He was what Thor should have looked like, although Chris Hemsworth was damn close.

A distant second, came Allie's words.

His leather jerkin, boots, and various straps and sheaths all creaked. Never, never could I have believed that creaking leather could sound and look so damn...

Easy, Sam. You have a boyfriend.

I know, I thought. *Care to finish for me?*

Never so damn hot!

"And how long has Squire Caleb been possessed?" Rory asked—or demanded—without breaking stride.

I tried to do the mental calculations, converting what I knew about the novel to this real-time situation. "About a month."

Sir Rory paused, cocked his head a little, which sent a splash of white hair cascading over his right shoulder. "That is about right. The stupid fool. Knights do not dabble in black magic. No doubt he did it for a woman."

The queen turned to me. "Are you witches? Please, I need to know."

"Yes and no, Your Highness."

"I see. Were you or were you not sent in answer to my prayers?"

"That is an emphatic *yes*."

"You are not angels?"

I shook my head.

"Dark angels, perhaps," said Allison.

"I see," said the queen, although I doubted she did. "But you are here to help me find my baby girl?"

"We are. And we will."

"And you are leading me to the dungeons?"

"Yes."

"Why?"

I looked at Allie, she looked at me. Together, we said, "Because that's where your daughter is being held."

She put a hand over her mouth. The look on her face suggested that she was both horrified and relieved. After all, her daughter was nearby.

"But where in the dungeons?" she asked. "They are vast—"

She paused, and her hand went up over her mouth again.

I said nothing, suspecting the queen had puzzled out where her daughter was being kept.

"We must hurry, then."

I couldn't have agreed more.

***

We were in the dungeons, having passed many cells and levels, most of which held lean and blood-ied men, although a few contained women. When they recognized their queen, they threw themselves against the bars and begged for mercy. She ignored them all.

Allison's expression might have been more horrified than my own. The dungeons appealed to the demoness within me, as, I suspected, she had seen—and used—her fair share of them. I knew she and other dark masters had worked with kings and queens of yesteryear to wage secret wars. I could only imagine how many good men and women had been tortured under Elizabeth's watch. A distant laughing that seemed to rise up from my deepest psyche suggested I'd hit upon a truth.

Crazy bitch, I thought, although I couldn't deny the allure of the dungeon system. Here, there were no rights, no rules, no respect for life. Here, people were brought to be tortured and to be killed.

Interesting, I thought. *Very interesting.*

Not interesting, Sam. Get a hold of yourself.

The idea of feasting upon a prisoner, a man or woman who had nowhere to run or hide, was growing inside me. I'd never seen such conditions before. At least, not in this life, and it was causing a nearly uncontrollable stirring—

And that's when I felt an ungodly smack upside my head.

"Snap out of it," said Allison in my ear. "Not joking. We save her baby, and we get out, and you get yourself home to your packets of blood."

"Fine," I said.

The dungeons had many levels, each seemingly worse than the last. The prisoners' screams grew louder, the begging more desperate, the torture devices more deplorable (and interesting). Desperate cries and ragged whimpering filled the air. Not to mention, the deeper we got, the creepier the dungeon masters became, many of whom watched us from holes in the wall, surrounded by their bloodied and arcane tools of the trade. I saw lots of spikes, gears, blades and stone grinders. I was buzzing, and it was all I could do to not run my tongue along one of those bloodied gears.

Eww, Sam. Just eww.

One dungeon master looked up, then bowed deeply when he saw our entourage. The queen merely nodded at him. I noted he had been sharpening what appeared to be a collar of spikes. Incidentally, the spikes were projected inward. I found this more interesting than I should have.

Focus, Sam.

The deeper we got, the darker the dungeons became. Rory snatched a torch from a wall sconce, and, shortly, we left even the dungeons behind. Rory seemed to know the way, and we all followed him. My own eyes had adjusted nicely, and I could see the never-ending flow of energy illuminating the air. Many tunnel offshoots branched off, but Rory confidently led the way down what appeared to be a main tunnel.

The tunnel dead-ended at another flight of stone steps, these seemingly danker and slipperier than the others. He reached back and took the queen's hand, leaving Allison and me to our own devices. I couldn't help but note the way both Rory's and the queen's fingers intertwined. Allison caught it too in the dancing torchlight. What Allison didn't catch was the way their two auras sort of blended together to form one big aura. These two were in love, and I suspected things were about to get juicy if Charlie would ever finish the damn book.

The stairs led down into another hallway, this one seemingly forgotten and narrower than the others. I noted that Sir Rory's shoulders nearly spanned the entire hallway. I might have noted this with far more curiosity than Kingsley would have appreciated.

Luckily, the narrow tunnel widened considerably, which did wonders for my claustrophobia. Many more tunnels branched this way and that, some, oddly angling down and up, at such degrees that a human would probably either tumble out of them and skid straight down.

Remember the dungeon dragon? Allie asked me, her telepathic words reaching only me.

I nearly snapped my fingers, until I remembered just how fierce the creature was that patrolled these nether regions. Indeed, upon closer inspection, I could see what very easily could have been claw marks... and burn marks. Yes, here be dragons.

Soon the main tunnel ended in a pile of boulders, and I knew, from having read the book, exactly where we were. The Cursed Dungeon. Here, the ceiling had also dropped, forcing the big knight to duck. He seemed irritable.

"This is it," said Sir Rory.

"Are you sure she is here, Lady Tam Tam?" asked the queen. She haltingly touched the closest boulder with her palm.

"Aye," I said, then, after seeing Allie's disapproving glare, I cleared my throat and said, "Yes."

"And you know this how, sorceress?" asked Rory.

"Technically," I said, jabbing a thumb at Allison, "she's closer to being a sorceress than I am—"

A low growl cut me off. I couldn't help but note that Rory's massive hands were laced with scars. I also noted the hands were opening and closing. If I had to guess, they were itching to close around my neck, or the hilt of his sword. Either way, my ass was in trouble.

Allison jumped in. "We were so told by the Creator."

"You throw the Lord's name out often, little shadow. How can we trust you?"

Little Shadow, thought Allison. *I like it!*

"They emerged from the wardrobe," said Queen Autumn, stepping away from the wall and dusting off her hands.

"Did they now?" asked Rory.

"They did, and you will have to trust me, my knight. They have answers. I feel it. Especially, here in this place."

I snapped my fingers. "The Good Magician Canterbury."

Rory arched an eyebrow. "You know much for a stranger."

I ignored him. Or, rather, I ignored him *cautiously*. I said, "The Good Magician Canterbury was found dead at the same time the princess was discovered missing." In the World of Dur, only the Good Magician Canterbury had access to the cursed dungeon.

"Perhaps he was coerced into opening the gate," said the queen, "just before he was murdered."

She was close. The good magician had, in fact, been blackmailed. After all, the Foul Wizard Xander had proof—supplied from Caleb Squire—that the good magician wasn't so good, after all. That he'd made a pact with the Dark One. A pact that gave the court magician nearly unstoppable power. I told them as much.

"He was blackmailed, then, to open the dungeon," asked Sir Rory.

"Yes," I said, although I really, really wanted to say *aye*.

The knight looked at his queen. "The spell," he said simply.

I knew of the spell, of course—any reader would have known that the princess had a protection spell placed on her by the Good Magician Canterbury, who really was good, even if he had a dark past. The spell ensured she would live to a ripe old age.

"And so Xander did the next best thing—he sealed her away in the Cursed Dungeon. With a sleeping spell."

"Thus giving him access to the throne," said Sir Rory. "By God, I will have his head!"

"In due time, my knight. First..."

"Yes, of course, my queen. First, we must find the babe. But how?"

I knew from Charlie's draft of the book that the cell was called impenetrable for a reason. Access to it was only available through magical means. Last I checked, Allison was about as magical as they came. But she shook her head when she picked up my thoughts.

I am, and I'm not, Sam. My skills are power skills. I can blast things. I can bind things with energy. I can illuminate things. I have no clue how to enchant something. Or how to break an enchantment. I've only been at this a few years, and, besides, I think we are dealing with a whole new magical system.

I nodded, thinking hard. *What if we went back to Charlie and asked him to edit the book, to write in a new description of the dungeon that isn't quite as impenetrable as everyone thinks?*

Allison shook her head. *I suspect he would merely create an alternative or parallel world, where another queen and another Rory are able to easily rescue her daughter. And if I know writers—*

You don't, Allie.

Well, from what I had gathered, they never like to make it easy on their characters. They like to throw a lot of shit at them, and watch their characters wade through it. It's fun for them as writers, and fun for readers.

Allison might have hit upon some truth. I thought: *So, in this draft of the story, the dungeon is impenetrable and the queen is screwed unless we can either resurrect the Good Magician Canterbury, or find another way into the dungeon.*

"You two are awfully quiet," said the queen. I wasn't very surprised to see Rory with his arm around her. I knew from the draft we had read that they had not yet been intimate, but they had been oh... so... close.

"They speak mindspeak, Your Highness," said Rory. "Have you not seen the way they look at each other? The little shadow even gestures sometimes, although no words are spoken."

I blinked, until I remembered *we* were the little shadows.

I'm not sure it's a compliment, Sam, thought Allie.

I shrugged, and the queen now spoke. "Yes, I see it now!"

"And what have you concluded, dark angels?" asked Rory, who, with his massive shoulders pressed up against the ceiling, looked a bit like Atlas carrying the weight of the world.

I spoke for the two of us. "We have concluded that Wench Allison is unable to break through to your daughter."

"Then we are without hope—"

"But," I said, cutting off a queen for the first time in my life, "I still have a few tricks up my sleeve."

32.

The end of the tunnel was little more than a pile of rocks.

That each and every rock had been created in the mind of my client was still something I was wrapping my own mind around. In a sense, I was inside Charlie's mind, interacting with his imagination. Then again, wasn't that the case with all writers? Weren't readers, in essence, taking a peek inside a writer's mind? And wasn't the writer taking the reader by the hand and leading them on a journey of the imagination? It was a special kind of relationship, the writer and reader, and it was its own form of telepathy.

Something banged from somewhere above us. Indeed, dust sifted down from the ceiling.

Rory withdrew his blade. "The dungeon dragon

cometh," he said.

Hurry, Sam, thought Allison. *And if you haven't noticed, we're kind of trapped. And did he just say cometh?*

He did, and we were. Trapped that is.

I closed my eyes and cast out my thoughts in a wide net. I had attributed such skills to Elizabeth in the past, but now I suspected this skill was of my own soul's doing: an ability to see in all directions, through any substance, usually up to about twenty feet. Now, I scanned through the wall and saw, well, more rock. I scanned the far wall, then the near wall. Then moved up and down the tunnel, scanning, but seeing nothing but more rock. No pockets of anything, no hidden chamber.

I went back to the end of the tunnel and climbed up onto the pile of rocks, ducking just under the ceiling. The tunnel shook some more, and now actual pebbles broke loose from the ceiling. Yeah, something was coming all right. And that something was huge and nasty.

Here, I closed my eyes just as I heard the first roar. I gasped, lost my concentration, tried again, this time pressing my head against the rock. *There.* A faint glow. It looked, in fact, like a star in a night sky. Just the smallest hint of light among the bedrock.

"Allison," I said, scrambling down from the pile of boulders. "I need you to blast these rocks."

"Blast?" She tore her gaze away from the tunnel

entrance. Indeed, I could see movement in the far distance. Big movement. Rory stood his ground, with his sword out before him, the queen behind him.

"Yes. Obliterate the shit out of them. And while you're at it, blast some of the wall, too, I need more room."

"Okay, stand back. Everyone stand back."

Except the other two weren't really listening. Indeed, the fearless knight had moved forward further down the hall, now withdrawing his rapier. The two swords wouldn't be much against the dungeon dragon, if my memory of the beast within the pages was anything like the real deal.

My friend stepped forward and did something I wouldn't have thought of. The nearly invisible bubble that expanded from her raised hands was, in fact, a shield. It was, I was certain, her way of ensuring the tunnel didn't cave in. She caught my eye and nodded. Yes, I was right. Next, she stretched out her hands toward the back end of the tunnel, closed her eyes. Her lips moved in a silent prayer or an incantation, or maybe a little bit of both. Now, energy of a very different kind swirled around her hands. Golden and bright, and unlike anything I had ever seen from her. It stopped swirling and next seemed to pulse. Her arms shook as the balls of light, like mini-suns, seemed to be gathering energy, building, building...

This is gonna be a doozy, I thought, suddenly

thankful as hell for the bubble shield overhead.

A sound emanated from her hand, a sort of subsonic whine, like that of a jet engine. The sound grew steadily, and when nearly unbearable, two ungodly bright balls of light blasted from Allison's hands and exploded into the crumbling rock wall. That Allison herself wasn't launched backward from the sheer force coming out of her was a miracle in itself. In this case, Isaac Newton was dead wrong: for every force, there was most certainly not an equal and opposite reaction. At least, not when dealing with magic. I expected rock fragments to hurl in every direction. But not even a pebble.

"No, Sam," said Allison. "I worked with the rock's consciousness and asked it to change its basic elemental composition."

"Um, what?" I asked, turning around to see a puff of what could only be described as... steam?

"A cloud, to be exact," said Allison.

"You turned the rock into a cloud?"

"Well, water, and yes. The elements rearranged themselves for me."

"Because you asked them to?"

"In a way. I also provided them the necessary energy to perform the transmutation—"

"The dragon, she comes!" shouted Rory.

We turned and saw it now: a hulking beast that veritably filled the tunnel to capacity, slithering along like a great subterranean snake. Indeed, I knew from Charlie's description that the dragon had, in fact, evolved to move through the tunnels much like a serpent.

"My queen," said Rory, dropping to a knee and taking her hand. "I will protect you until my last dying breath."

As Rory rose and dashed down the tunnel, I said to Allison, "Go help Sir Loincloth. We don't need him fried to a crisp. Last I checked, he's the hero in the story. We can talk about the rock-to-water thing later."

She grinned, turned, and raced off down the tunnel behind Rory. Already, I could see the energy forming around her hands. This time, a pale yellow energy. An energy, I knew, that meant business.

I turned once again to what had been a boulder-strewn end of the tunnel. Now it was something else, entirely. It was a tunnel that went deeper into the rock formation. I looked at the queen, and she looked at me, not sure what to do. I took her hand and said, "C'mon. It's probably safer with me."

33.

We headed deeper into the freshly blasted tunnel.

Not too much deeper, granted, but certainly deep enough to put a little distance between us and the ungodly racket going on out there.

You okay out there? I asked.

The dragon is magical, Sam. It can deflect my best stuff.

Okay, sounds like you have it under control.

But I just said—

She growled just as I signed off. Then again, it might have been the dragon growling, too. Either way, with Conan the Barbarian and the Wicked Witch of the West out there, I was pretty sure the dragon had its claws full.

I focused on the task at hand, which just so

happened to be saving a baby from an eternity of prison. Although the tunnel had been hollowed out by some pretty cool witchcraft, and most of the walls were as smooth as a baby's butt, that didn't stop bigger rocks and clumps of dirt from dropping free from the ceiling with each explosion or thump from out in the hallway. I might be immortal, which means I would survive a cave-in. Which also meant I could be buried for an eternity, which sounded terrible.

"What do we do, Lady Tam Tam?" asked the queen.

I gave her credit. She sounded far stronger and calmer than she probably had any right to be.

"I have a plan. Kinda."

"I am not familiar with this word, 'kinda.'"

"It means it's not a quite a plan."

"Ah, well, not quite a plan is better than no plan at all," said the queen, and no truer words had ever been spoken.

With the queen huddled close and smelling of something completely foreign to me—a sort of sweet sage mixed with sea salt, undoubtedly what passed for perfume in this strange land—I closed my eyes and rested my palms on the stone. What I saw nearly knocked my socks off. Or my Asics. I had been expecting to see more rock, and maybe a fragment of light.

This time, I saw so much more.

34.

It was an open space, but just barely.

A man could sit in there, but not stand. A man could lie in there, but not fully. It was a hellish sort of prison, one that was entirely surrounded by many dozens, perhaps even hundreds, of layers of rock. In the ceiling, I could see vent holes, undoubtedly reaching the surface, perhaps even magically so. There was no door, no bed, no table, no stool. Only a small pocket of rock from which to suffer.

Sam, we can't hold it off for much longer...

I nodded, then said to the queen, "I'll be right back."

"But where are you—"

Except I had already summoned the single flame, and within it, I saw the tiny stone cell. Most important, I saw what was hovering in the tiny cell:

a baby girl, suspended in the air, and surrounded by blue light.

In a blink, I was gone.

***

I found myself on my back, within the stone chamber, and looking up at the hovering babe, wrapped in a dangling white shawl. Interestingly, my inner alarm sounded, buzzing just inside my right ear.

The little girl had been clearly enchanted; indeed, I could see the blue light pulsating around her. I suspected that same enchantment could, potentially, ensnare me. Warning heard and heeded.

I carefully eased myself up, avoiding the blue glow at all costs. There was barely enough room for me to sit up, much less navigate around the floating babe. Truly, this was a place for prisoners to go mad. I seriously questioned Charlie Reed's own sanity. I mean, who thinks up these places?

Most interesting was the silence. The eternal silence. The complete and total and all-consuming silence. It was as if this place had never known sound. Even the sound of my own breathing or beating heart would have been something, anything. My heart beat, I knew, but only rarely. Which got me thinking... the baby? Was she breathing? Surely, I would have heard her by now, in this small and cramped and silent place.

I sat up on my knees, all too aware that the ceiling itself was just a few feet away. Already, I was feeling the panic settling in. This place... was just too much, even for a vampire. Especially for a vampire.

The babe was a foot or so away from me. The soft blue edges of the light nearly reached me. Correction, some of the azure wisps floated around my shoulder, and as they did... as they did... I felt the sleepiness take over. I also heard the warning bell, buzzing louder and louder. But I ignored the buzzing, the stupid, incessant buzzing. Why wouldn't Mom just let me sleep in this one time? Stupid alarm, stupid mom, stupid school.

I forced open my eyes, but a literal weight pushed them down again. A heavy, relaxing, beautiful weight, peaceful weight...

Yes, sleeping now felt so right, so perfect, even while my friend was fighting for her life, and while a mother waited anxiously in the tunnel beyond for any news about her kidnapped baby. Yes, a nap—a long, dark, blissful nap—wouldn't hurt anyone, right?

SAM!! WAKE UP!!

Allie, shhh, it's quiet time...

It's the sleeping spell, Sam!! WAKE UP!!

Allie, please, you'll wake the baby.

Move back, Sam!! Move back NOW!!!

Will it make me more comfortable if I move back a few inches, Allie? I sure am tired. It's been a long day...

Sure, Sam. Whatever. Move back a few inches and then you can sleep for as long as you want.

Okay, Allie. You sure are a swell friend. Needy, but still a swell friend.

I moved back an inch or two and was preparing to sleep, perhaps forever, when my eyes popped open. I looked around, confused, wondering where the hell I was, until I saw the babe, the blue light, and the rock cage around me.

I gasped and inched back some more, hitting my head on the rock wall behind me. The pain helped to further jar me awake, and snap me back to my senses.

Welcome back, Sam, came Allison's voice in my head. *Now, please hurry. The dragon has figured out all our tricks and is advancing.*

Before me, the sweet little girl, no older than a year or so, slept with an angelic expression on her face, as she would do for, perhaps, forever, unless I figured something out. What if I leaped in with guns blazing, so to speak, grabbed the girl, and teleported back before I fell asleep? Maybe, but I suspected that much exposure to the spell would instantly conk me out.

An explosion rocked the tiny cell and I heard a distant scream in my head, followed by a god-awful roar.

Think, Sam. Think.

I considered my very limited options. There was

nothing in the cell to use in order to reach out to the baby, something that could be used as, say, a buffer between me and the blue light. A shepherd's staff would have been awesome right about now.

And then I had it, and nearly squealed. I immediately took off my shirt and one of my shoes.

It didn't take me long at all to tie the laces of my Asics to the cuff of my long-sleeved shirt.

All too aware that I was wearing only a sports bra in a magical dungeon far beneath a castle in a fantasy land created in the mind of my client, I positioned myself as close to the sleeping babe as I could without contacting the amorphous blue light.

"Here goes nothing," I said, and gently tossed the shoe out and over the floating bundle. I was prepared to leap forward should, say, the babe fall like a rock, jarred loose from its hovering orbit. But she didn't fall, and the shoe and shirt passed over the sleeping girl, through the blue light, to dangle near the floor. She remained floating, and I now had a "safety line" around her, and, most important, I wasn't feeling the very real need to take the mother of all cat naps.

Admittedly, I'd been worried that the magic spell, as evidenced by the blue glow, would snake along my shoe and shirt and envelop me, too. But it didn't. The light merely stayed a constant, nor did the babe stir. And so I did the only thing I could think of: I dropped back to the floor and stomach-crawled, Navy SEAL-like, on my belly until my outstretched fingers could snag my shoe, which I did after a few swipes. Once done, I retreated to where I'd started: off to one side of the sleeping princess, but now I was holding my shirt in one hand and my tied-off shoe in the other. The rest of the contraption was lassoed safely around the babe.

Good enough, I thought.

Sam! Sir Rory is injured! Hurry!

I gave the tee-shirt lasso a tug, and the fabric tightened around the babe. And something else happened, too: the tiny sleeping figure shifted a little. Like a kite altering course in mid-air. I gave the makeshift fishing net another tug, and the little girl drifted some more, this time toward me. Most important, she drifted *out of* the blue haze. I had been afraid the spell would follow her, but it didn't. In fact, it was doing the opposite. The more the babe moved, the more the blue glow dissipated.

The princess was now drifting toward me, a tiny, tethered dirigible in the sky—

And that's when she dropped like a rock.

Luckily, my reflexes are faster than any dropping rock, and both my hands shot out and caught her before she was even halfway to the floor.

Most important, the glowing blue sleeping spell was gone. I knew this because the sweetheart opened her eyes, took one look at me... and screamed bloody murder.

Despite her wailing, I grinned and summoned the single flame.

35.

Queen Autumn screamed when I appeared, and screamed again when I handed over her wailing baby.

Next, I dashed out of the freshly blasted tunnel, splashed through puddles of what had once been solid rock, and emerged into the main tunnel system, where I saw something that would have and should have turned my bowels into water. But it didn't. Not here, and not now.

A wingless, massive, scaled dragon, with claws the size of a Mini Cooper, was presently hovering over my witchy friend who, herself, was hovering over the fallen knight, who was bleeding profusely from a terrible head wound.

So much blood...

Allie held the knight with one arm, while her

other arm was raised above her. She had created what appeared to be a very feeble, nearly invisible shield. Meanwhile, the dragon alternately blasted it with jets of fire and raked at it with claws long enough to disembowel an elephant.

Without breaking stride, I summoned the flame again—and this time, saw Talos within it. He seemed eager to come, if that was possible.

And now I was suddenly much bigger than I was before, and the roar that erupted from my mouth was deafening even to my own ears. The wingless serpent snapped its great triangular head up—and if a dragon could look startled, I was seeing it now. It took a step and cocked its head, no doubt surprised as hell at seeing me now. As I advanced, it continued stepping back.

My presence also got Allie's attention, and now she dropped both hands around the fallen knight, summarily losing her feeble shield. She didn't need her shield. She had me now, and, as the dragon continued retreating, I stepped carefully over my brave friend and the fallen knight.

I knew from experience that summoning fire took a little time. It wasn't just something a dragon had, literally, at the tip of his tongue. It had to be generated from down deep, within a special furnace in his lungs. And I felt it generating now, building, building...

Hurry Talos.

Almost ready, Sam, I heard him say in my mind.

Meanwhile, the creature before me stopped its retreat altogether, reared back, and shot a super-heated jet of molten death at me. I did all I could do, and ducked behind Talos's massive wings. I knew instinctively that his wings could only survive so many such attacks. Indeed, the burn I felt was excruciating, and I found myself apologizing profusely to the creature who'd lent me his body. And just when the dragon before us reared back to fire a second blast, an attack that might just burn Talos's precious wings to a crisp, I heard the words I was waiting to hear:

Ready, Sam.

Breathing fire always felt a bit, well, orgasmic. And I was sure this was the case even now, except this time I didn't notice. What I did notice was the welling of energy in my chest. What I did notice was that something magical—something alchemical—was happening inside of me. Air was turning to fire, much as the rock had turned to water.

The four elementals, I thought briefly.

Yes, Sam, I heard Talos say, and then I wasn't listening to anyone or anything else, for now, something great was burning for release. And release I did, opening my mouth wide and thrusting my head forward: a great explosion of fire erupted out of me, searing Talos's throat and mouth and tongue and lips. I knew that after each burst of fire, the big fellow had to recuperate and heal. Breathing fire wasn't something he did every day—only when needed. And these days, it was mostly needed by *me.*

Luckily, my flying friend could also heal rather quickly. Maybe I had that effect on him. I didn't know.

But for now, fire shot forth down the underground tunnel, roiling and twisting and lapping. The wingless dragon let loose with a blast of its own, but, I suspected, its own fire had mostly been spent, if that was possible.

It's possible, Sam, came Talos's thoughts.

Which was a good thing in this case, too, for Talos's own blast overcame the dungeon dragon's effort, and soon the fire—fire that was still erupting from my now-burning lips—encompassed the creature completely.

As its own flame sputtered out, the creature twisted its now-glowing head this way and that. It clawed the air, screeching. The ungodly, hideous, ear-piercing screech wasn't of this earth. Literally. Most important, it retreated. And by retreating, it did something that seemed to defy physics: it turned in place, contorting its fluid, apparently boneless body. My last image was of its still-smoking tail as it dashed away.

Did I just have an honest-to-god dragon fight? I asked.

You did, Sam.

With the dragon gone, I thanked Talos and

returned to my human form—and was as naked as the day I was born. I saw the queen running toward us. She had missed the show, I think, which was probably for the best. What couldn't be missed was that I was now butt-naked. Luckily, the injured Rory occupied most of her attention.

Once we were together again, I took hold of the baby's little hand in my own and placed another on Rory's bent back. I told the others to grab one of my shoulders. The queen did, looking confused as hell. I didn't blame her one bit.

Especially when we all reappeared in the forgotten little room with the magical wardrobe.

***

Sir Rory had met the business end of one of the dragon's claws.

Allie had used a bit of her magic to cauterize the wound enough to keep it from bleeding out. But there was more going on here than just the open wound and resulting internal damage. The skin had turned a bit green and looked, if anything, rotten. Although the bleeding had stopped, the poison seemed to be spreading. Myself, I was covered in a sheet that now formed a shawl. I was going to miss those Asics.

With Sir Rory still propped in Allison's lap— and her own clothing covered in blood and the queen nearby clutching her baby—I found the closest sentry and compelled him to fetch a healer, a number of whom, according to the queen, resided within the castle.

A short time later, I led the portly man back into the queen's private chamber. Once there, the man's eyes nearly bugged out of his head when he spotted the kidnapped princess returned once again to her mother. He nearly asked about the babe, until he saw the realm's greatest knight lying injured in Allison's arms.

The physician magician asked for a pillow, which I fetched, and soon the big knight was lying on the stone floor, just a few feet in front of the wardrobe. The healer asked for some space, and we all gave it to him, including the queen. I next watched a series of potions being produced from the folds of the man's robe. Many of them bubbled and steamed. He mixed a number of them together into a smaller vial, stopped it with a cork, shook the hell out of it, then uncorked it and poured the contents over the knight's wounded head. Steam hissed. Green steam, and Sir Rory spasmed and roared, and then fell silent.

Later, the physician came to us and took the queen aside. I saw him look at us as he spoke, and she shook her head sternly and he nodded. After that, a number of solemn knights appeared and took their fallen leader away, off to the castle infirmary. Word was, the big guy would probably make it, although the poison might have lasting effects.

Rory, I suspected, was tough enough and big enough—and in love enough with the queen—to power through and still be damned near the greatest knight the realm had ever seen. Earlier, there had been a brief, quiet moment when the physician had stepped out to fetch the knights, when the queen found herself mostly alone with Sir Rory. Mostly, because Allie and I were standing off to the side. The queen had leaned over him and patted his great chest and kissed him softly on the cheek. The knight had smiled.

Now, we were alone with the queen and her babe, which she had, up to this point, refused to let go of. I didn't blame her. In her world, the babe had been gone for two weeks. Far, far too long. How she hadn't gone insane with worry, I didn't know.

"I am forever grateful to the two of you," said the queen, although she didn't take her eyes off the cooing babe, which was now wide-eyed and eager. She should be; after all, she had taken a helluva long nap.

I nearly said: *All in a day's work for dark angels, Your Highness.* That is, until I heard how lame it sounded in my own head.

Allie said, "All in a day's work for dark angels, Your Highness."

Well, I think it sounds cute. She smirked.

Oh, brother.

"Dark angels, indeed." She looked at Allie. "I saw what you did in the tunnel. And I saw how you protected Rory. And you." She turned to me. "You disappeared before my eyes, and reappeared holding my baby, wrapped in your shirt and, oddly, your shoe."

I said, "Long story."

"You needed to stay clear of the sleeping spell," said the queen. "And use both articles of clothing as a noose."

"Maybe not so long, after all."

"Very ingenious, Lady Tam Tam." She kept her eyes on me. "When I emerged out of the tunnel, I next watched something incredible."

I waited, wondering if I should remove this memory from her mind, but decided to let it play out a little further. She said, "I watched a woman turn into a winged dragon."

"Any chance you imagined that?" I asked.

She smiled at me warmly, which was odd. Surely, she should have been alarmed, or terrified. Then again, she did live in a magical realm, complete with dungeon dragons, wizards, ice trolls, you name it! I could only imagine the other wonders that awaited beyond the castle walls... and in Charlie's extensive notes.

"No, Lady Tam Tam. I saw it with mine own eyes."

I said, "We did what we had to do to save your daughter."

She kept her gaze on me. "Will I see you again?"

"Mayhap you will," I said.

"We're just a prayer away," piped in Allie.

Geez, Allie. Could you sound any lamer?

Sorry. I couldn't help myself. But she didn't sound sorry, even in my head. I didn't have to be telepathic to know she liked being considered a dark angel. And that we had been grouped together as a sort of team.

Admit it, you like it too.

No, I don't.

You could even say we're Charlie's Dark Angels.

Good God, I thought. *You went there.*

I did. And I will do it again.

The queen looked at both of us, a small smile on her face, seemingly aware of our telepathic tit-for-tat. She adjusted her hold on her mewling babe, whose little hands were reaching up through the fabric to play with the queen's curly locks. I next did the only thing I could think of: I bowed.

Now who looks lame, thought a giggling Allison, as she bowed along with me.

Oh, shut up.

The queen hugged both of us with her free hand and didn't try to stop the tears from flowing. I gave the little booger in her arms a kiss as well, and then led the way into the wardrobe.

Once there, Allie took my hand, and, together, we stepped back through the wardrobe.

36.

Allie stumbled into me, and I stumbled into her.

"Is that how it feels when you teleport?" she asked, holding me.

"A bit," I said. "Except I usually don't have a big fat foot standing on mine."

"Oops, sorry."

"Welcome back you two," said Charlie Reed, coming from around his desk, an exuberant look in his wild eyes.

I didn't have to read his mind to know what the man had been up to. "Let me guess: your writer's block is gone?"

"Gone, obliterated, and replaced with even more wild ideas. I can't stop them. All thanks to you."

"Er, how long have we been gone?" asked Allie.

"A couple hours. Maybe more. Speaking of

which, how did it go in there?"

"I think you know how it went in there," I said. "You've been writing ever since."

"Yes. The moment you two disappeared. And I mean exactly that: you two literally disappeared in a blink."

"And what happened while we were gone?" I pressed.

"The ideas flowed. And flowed and flowed. It was all I could do to keep up with them."

"And what did you write about?"

"Of the appearance of two dark angels who rescue the kidnapped princess."

"And did one of these dark angels turn into a dragon?" pressed Allie.

"And did Sir Rory suffer a near-fatal injury?" I added.

He looked at, then ran his fingers through his hair and stared at us. He looked, I suspected, a bit like Dr. Lichtenstein had looked when he had created his first successful monsters. "Why, yes. Is that... is that what happened in... there?" He pointed toward the hallway we had just stepped out of. Or stumbled out of.

"It was," I said.

"But... but I had one such dark angel be, in fact, a vampire. And the other, a witch."

This is freaking me out, Sam, thought Allison.

Me, too.

And so we stood like that for a few more

seconds, each wondering who had influenced whom. Truth was, I really didn't want to know.

Charlie motioned toward our phones on the nightstand. "Both have been buzzing non-stop for the past twenty minutes. I hope everything is okay."

I really, really hated when my phone buzzed non-stop. A non-stop buzzing phone only meant one thing: bad news.

I approached it carefully, working out mentally where my kids were, and knowing they were safe with Kingsley. They had to be safe, right? It was Kingsley for crissakes.

I picked it up and saw that I had missed nine calls from Kingsley.

He had texted me no less than twenty times, too, most of which said the exact same thing: "Tammy's gone."

37.

I didn't live far from Charlie Reed's house, and I was home in minutes. Had Kingsley known where I was, he might have come to find me himself, although he'd also thought it best to stay home with Anthony. Not a bad idea.

Of course, I had done all I could not to panic. After all, this wasn't a brazen, midday kidnapping, as had been the case with my son. No, this was just a moody teenager ditching her babysitter. A baby-sitter with perfect hearing, mind you. A babysitter who would never, ever let her out of his sight without my permission. I could call Sherbet. And tell him what? That my daughter was missing for an hour? I couldn't pull him away from real police work for just that.

Kingsley met me at the door. His thick mane of

hair was askew. The look in his amber eyes was particularly wild. "She put me to sleep, Sam."

"But how?"

Despite all my best efforts, I heard the panic in my voice. Hearing the panic made me panic more.

While I ran through the house, searching her room, her closet, Anthony's room, Anthony's closet—my office, the garage, the backyard, Kingsley followed me and explained: "I was watching TV, and then I heard... something. A whispering. A soft whispering. It was... suggesting that I sleep."

"And did you?"

"I must have, Sam. When I opened my eyes again, she was gone." He produced a familiar phone. "Strangely, she left her cell phone."

I scrolled through it quickly, bypassing her password, which I had created for her. "No calls," I said. "No texts."

"Unless she deleted them," said Allison.

We were all standing in the living room. My son watched us from the hallway.

"Did she say anything to you, Anthony?"

"No, Mom."

"Did you see her leave?"

"I was sleeping, too."

I stood there in the living room as my world threatened to spin out of control, especially when I realized my sixteen-year-old freak of a daughter had somehow taught herself a brand-new trick. Or worse, someone had taught her mind control. And I damn well knew who that someone was.

Allie, who had been picking up my thoughts, said, "You can't be serious, Sam."

"Serious about what?" asked Kingsley, not privy to our mindspeak.

But I was serious, and I knew I wasn't wrong. I took in some worthless fucking air and discovered my fists were clenched.

"He has her," I said to no one in particular.

"Who has her?" asked Kingsley.

"The devil," I said. "And we're going to get her back."

The End

About the Author:

J.R. Rain is an ex-private investigator who now writes full-time. He lives in a small house on a small island with his small dog, Sadie. Please visit him at www.jrrain.com.

Made in the USA
Middletown, DE
22 May 2021

40209614R00156